HOT LEAD AND COLD NERVE

Center Point
Large Print

Also by Bradford Scott and available from Center Point Large Print:

Outlaw Land
Border War
Ranger Daring
Doom Trail
Border Blood
Guns of Bang Town
Trail of Blood and Bones
Rimrock Raiders
Bullets for a Ranger
Bullets Over the Border
Hot Lead

HOT LEAD AND COLD NERVE

A Walt Slade Western

Bradford Scott

Center Point Large Print
Thorndike, Maine

This Center Point Large Print edition
is published in the year 2024 by arrangement with
Golden West Inc.

Originally published in the US by Pyramid Books.

The text of this Large Print edition is unabridged.
In other aspects, this book may vary
from the original edition.
Printed in the United States of America
on permanent paper sourced using
environmentally responsible foresting methods.
Set in 16-point Times New Roman type.

ISBN: 979-8-89164-278-2

The Library of Congress has cataloged this record
under Library of Congress Control Number: 2024938329

1

"O, young Lochinvar is come out of the west,
Through all the wide Border his steed was the best!"

So sang Ranger Walt Slade, named by the Mexican *peónes* of the Rio Grande river villages, *El Halcón*—The Hawk—in his deep rich voice as he too rode out of the west, on the trail from Laredo to Brownsville.

"Doubt if Sir Walter Scott would be flattered by my rendering, and I don't put myself in the class of Lochinvar," Slade said to Shadow, his tall black horse, "but it sorta applies. We're riding out of the west, and this is certainly the Border, and I'll put you up against any cayuse in the Border country and play you to win."

Shadow snorted cheerful agreement and ambled on.

Meanwhile, Slade was regarding a clump of cattle grazing nearby.

"A Bar L burn," he remarked. "Don't recall seeing that brand before. What we're crossing right now is, or used to be, the Lazy P spread, old Potter Mays' ranch. Understood it was for sale. So now there's a new owner who has changed the brand, as Sheriff Calder mentioned in his letter to Captain Jim." He was referring to Captain Jim

McNelty, the famed commander of the Border Battalion of the Texas Rangers.

"Yes, a new owner who wasn't around the last time we were here," Slade resumed. "Well, next is Charge Grundy's B Cross C, then Ezekiel Combs' big holding, and then Brownsville where we should get a chance to put on the nosebag, which we can both stand by the time we arrive in that blasted hell-town, as Captain Jim calls it. So june along, horse, and stop complaining. You've had a few mouthfuls of grass on the way, which is more than I've had."

Shadow, who was not complaining, did not rise to the bait and moseyed on at a good pace, minus a snort.

Ahead, the trail wound through long and thick stands of chaparral which clothed the slopes running up gently on either side. As they progressed, the growth eased away from the trail somewhat, but was tall and even thicker further up the slopes and on the crests.

Shadow had jogged along for nearly a mile when Slade abruptly raised his head in an attitude of listening. From some distance to the front had come the unmistakable clang of a rifle shot. It was not repeated.

Slade rode on, very much on the alert, for in this section it behooved a lone rider to be watchful at all times, especially after such an ominous report. Constantly he studied the slopes and their crests, watching the movements of birds on the wing, which did not appear to be disturbed. He had covered perhaps a quarter of a mile when he suddenly reined in and sat staring ahead.

The dead man lay in the trail, his glazing eyes glaring up stonily at the deep blue of the Texas sky. Nearby, a saddled and bridled horse stood patiently. Slade noted the tie rope, and the throwing rope looped from the saddle. Evidently in life the fellow had been a cowhand.

For minutes Slade sat motionless, scanning the slopes and the crests with eyes that missed nothing, his amazingly keen hearing attuned to the slightest sound that would betray the presence of a lurking drygulcher. He saw nothing, heard nothing. Concluding there was nothing to fear, he dismounted and approached the body, which was that of a lanky but broad-shouldered and solidly built man with dark hair and eyes a florid complexion. He gently turned the body over on its face.

There was a bullet hole between the shoulder blades, a little to the left.

"Got him dead center; never knew what hit him," Slade muttered. "Well, guess it's another souvenir for Sheriff Calder."

Without apparent effort, he picked up the heavy form and draped it over the saddle of the waiting horse, securing it in place with tie ropes. Then he remounted Shadow and rode on, leading the other horse. He had covered another half a mile or so when again he raised his head in an attitude of listening. From beyond a brush-screened bend of the trail, a hundred yards ahead, was sounding the beat of fast hoofs. Another moment and half a dozen horsemen in rangeland clothes bulged around the bend and jerked their mounts to a halt, staring. Slade rode to meet them.

Suddenly one exclaimed, "That's Duke's horse!"

"Good God! And that's Duke tied to the saddle!" yelped another. Hands darted to holsters.

Then the hands were motionless, their owners rigid. For they were staring into the hungry black muzzles of two long guns that had apparently come from nowhere.

Slade spoke, his voice soft, musical, but edged with a deadly menace, "Anybody in the notion of fanging? If so, get going; I aim to accommodate."

Nobody appeared inclined to accept the suggestion. For a moment there was silence. Then one man spoke, a tall, lean but broad-shouldered individual with a hard-lined face that Slade thought rather ruggedly good looking. He had slightly grizzled hair and pale-blue eyes.

"Where did you find him, feller?" he asked.

"About half a mile back," Slade answered.

"Did—did you—shoot him?"

"And if I did, of course I'd be packing him to town and Sheriff Calder," Slade replied. "Were you fellows all behind the cellar door when they were handing out brains?"

Under the contempt in the Ranger's voice, the bunch flushed and looked foolish.

"Guess this feller's talking straight," said the lean man, in an altered voice. "Tom Calder *is* the sheriff. Did you see who shot him?" Slade shook his head, and abruptly holstered his guns with the same blinding speed with which he had drawn them.

"I heard the rifle report," he replied, "but I was quite a way to the west. I'd say he was shot from the crest of the rise, or anyhow from some distance. The bullet is still in him, which would not have been the case were he shot from close range. Who is he?"

"One of my hands," the other said bitterly. "A good man."

Slade asked another question, "You own this land?"

"That's right," the other answered.

"Name's Lanham, I believe," Slade said.

"That's right," the lean man repeated, looking surprised. "How come you learned it?"

"From a letter Sheriff Calder wrote," Slade replied, not mentioning to whom the letter had been written.

"I see," said Lanham. His face flushed darkly red with anger as he gazed at the body. "Those blankety-blank B Cross C devils!" he growled.

“What makes you think the Charge Grundy outfit is responsible for the death of your rider?” Slade asked.

“We’ve had trouble with them,” Lanham explained. “Grundy claims a slice of my holding. We dispute it. His hellions and my boys had quite a ruckus in town a little while back. We gave ’em as good as they sent.”

“I see,” Slade said. “And instead of allowing the courts to settle the dispute in a lawful manner, you are both taking the law in your own hands. Not a wise thing to do.”

Lanham muttered and mumbled but did not argue the point. “We’ve lost cows, too,” he said defiantly.

Slade tried a shot in the dark. “And I suppose Grundy also claims to have lost cows?”

“Yes, he does,” Lanham admitted, adding, “but I don’t believe the horned toad. He would claim that.”

“And quite likely he says the same of you,” Slade observed. “With the chance you could both be wrong. Well, this palaver isn’t getting us anywhere, so I’m heading for Brownsville and the sheriff. I think it would be a good notion for you to come along.”

When Lanham hesitated, Slade drew something from his pocket and held it for the other to see. It was a deputy sheriff’s badge.

“I have several times in the past been Tom

Calder's special deputy, and I think I still am," he explained. "So I believe it would be a good idea if you did as I say."

"Well, if you put it that way, I reckon you're right," Lanham conceded. "Don't want to arg'fy with the Law."

Suddenly his crooked teeth flashed white in a grin. "And you pack a sorta authority I figure it ain't healthy to arg'fy with," he added.

For the first time during the passage, Slade smiled, the flashing white smile of *El Halcón* which men, and women, found irresistible. Lanham and his hands also smiled.

"Well, I suppose we'd better get moving if my horse and myself are ever going to get in line for the nosebag," Slade suggested. Lanham nodded and they got under way.

"We'll be on Grundy's land in a little," Lanham remarked. "Hope we don't run into his hellions. I'd rather not have any more trouble today."

"You won't," Slade promised grimly.

"Grundy and his bunch know you, eh?" said the Bar L owner.

"They do," Slade replied briefly.

"Then I reckon we ain't got anything to bother about," Lanham said.

2

Without incident they crossed both Grundy's and Ezekiel Combs' holdings and as the Texas sunset was flaming its multicolored splendor in the west, they reached Brownsville on the Rio Grande and made their way to the sheriff's office.

Lanham and his men tenderly lifted their dead bunky from the saddle and bore him into the office, Slade following.

Sheriff Calder was at his desk. He stared, leaped to his feet.

"Well, I'll be hanged!" he exploded. "Might have knowed it, might have knowed it. The minute *El Halcón* drops in the section, trouble starts!"

Lanham and the others stared; evidently they had heard that name before.

"*El Halcón*!" Lanham repeated in an awed voice. "Great holy sufferin' cats! And I sorta figured to pull on him!"

"Understand bad people have it sorta tough in the Hereafter," was Calder's only comment. Lanham "got it."

"All right," said the sheriff. "Let's have it. Who plugged this feller, and why?"

"Unfortunately, we have no definite answer to

either question," Slade replied, and related what he knew of the happening. The sheriff favored Lanham with an accusing glower.

"And I suppose you hellions blame Charge Grundy and his hands, eh?"

"Well, we did, at first," Lanham admitted, "but now we sorta ain't so sure."

"Slade gave you a talking to, eh?"

"Yes, guess he did," Lanham conceded, gazing at the tall Ranger. "Somehow he made us see things sorta different."

"Uh-huh, he has a habit of making folks see things—his way," Calder commented dryly.

"Guess that's right, too," Lanham agreed. "Well, reckon we might as well amble over to the Blue Bell and tie onto something to eat and a snort or two before heading home. Anything more to say about poor Duke Ambrose, Sheriff?"

"We'll hold an inquest for the poor devil and try and run down the sidewinder that killed him," replied Calder.

"And I've a notion you will, now," said Lanham, with another glance at Slade. "Come on, boys."

"Just a minute," Slade said. "You haven't told me how Duke happened to be riding where he was and where you must have been shortly before."

"He was rounding up some strays from the thickets this side of Grundy's holding," Lanham answered. "The rest of us were digging out a waterhole a mite farther to the west. We hadn't seen him since morning."

"Guess you fellers had better be in for the inquest Doc will be wanting to hold tomorrow afternoon," the sheriff put in.

"Okay, we'll be here," Lanham promised. "Let's go, boys."

After the door had closed, Calder said, referring to Dixon Lanham, "Well, what do you think of him?"

"Frankly, I don't know," Slade replied. "He's no fool, of that I'm convinced. His men are salty, no doubt as to that, and above the average in intelligence. I'll have to hold my judgment in abeyance until I learn more about him."

The sheriff nodded at the blanket-covered body on the floor. "Sometimes fellers get themselves killed for talking out of turn," he observed meaningfully.

"Yes, but we have no proof that is the case here," Slade said. "So don't go jumping at conclusions. Remember, you looked sideways at Grundy for a while after he coiled his twine here, and he turned out to be okay. If that fellow had been killed in a fair, stand-up fight, I might be inclined to give a little thought to Grundy and his bunch, for they're all the quick-tempered, chip-on-the-shoulder brand. But Duke was without a doubt drygulched by somebody holed up in the brush, which I would say lets out Grundy and his hands."

"I wouldn't argue that," Calder conceded. "Well, now what?"

"Now I'm stabling my horse and then to the Blue Bell for a bite to eat," Slade decided. "Beginning to feel a mite lank."

"Okay, I'll go along," said Calder. "About time for me to tie onto a surrounding, too."

The Mexican stable keeper remembered Slade and his horse and had a warm greeting for both. Shadow, usually a one-man horse who seldom allowed anybody to put a hand on him without his master's sanction, apparently remembered the keeper, greatly to his delight, and offered no objections to being led to a stall and to having his rig removed.

"Fear not, *Capitán*," the keeper said to Slade. "Only the best for him. It is the honor great to serve *El Halcón* and his wonderful *caballo*. The vacant stall? Ha! The Señorita Dolores Malone has already ridden to work in Amado Menendez' cantina in Matamoros, so the stall is empty. Perhaps *Capitán* remembers Dolores, *si*?" he added, with a twinkle in his black eyes.

"Seems to me I sort of recall somebody by that name," Slade admitted. Both the keeper and the sheriff chuckled loudly.

As Shadow was in safe hands, Slade and the sheriff repaired to the big Blue Bell restaurant and saloon, where lean, lanky, and saturnine Fats Boyer, the owner, also had a warm greeting for Slade.

"Don't bother to order," he said as he led them to a table near the dance floor, from which there was a good view of the door and the windows, and most of the room as reflected in the mirror behind the bar. "Just put away what the kitchen boys dish up when they learn *El Halcón* is here. I'll fetch drinks. Everything on the house."

He proceeded to bring drinks and then hurried to the kitchen to inform the help, all Mexicans, that *El Halcón* was present and to stir their stumps accordingly.

"Here we go again!" moaned the sheriff. "Pounds and more pounds! Eatin' with you is a calamity."

However, despite his lament, he put away everything that was, a little later, placed before him.

Dixon Lanham and his hands were at the bar, drinking and conversing with acquaintances, so Slade kept an eye on the swinging doors, for he did not propose to have a row cut loose between the two outfits if Charge Grundy and his hands put in an appearance.

However, nothing untoward seemed to be happening and he and Calder proceeded to enjoy their really excellent meal in peace.

Finally Slade ordered a last cup of steaming coffee, leaned back in his chair, and rolled a cigarette. With the brain tablet functioning properly, he glanced at the sheriff. "So suppose you give me the lowdown on conditions here," he suggested.

"Oh, nothing so very new or different from the other times you were here," Calder replied. "Owlhoots roaming the brush country and showing up from across the river. Quite a bit of cow stealing, handled mighty smart. Two stores robbed right here in town; owner of one killed, knife stuck in his back. Some shootings over in Matamoros. One on the bridge. Folks over here heard lead whistle from that one. Which ain't the first time, of course."

Slade commented on the last statement. "Does that mean there is liberator trouble south of the Rio Grande?"

Calder shrugged his shoulders. "Can't say for sure," he replied, "but there are whispers, or so I've been told. Wouldn't be surprised if Amado Menendez can tell you more about that. Oh, yes, a couple of stage holdups to help things along."

"Begins to look a little like there's an organized outfit working the section," Slade remarked.

"I sorta lean to that notion," the sheriff conceded. "Everything that's happened has been handled mighty smooth."

"How long has all this been going on?" Slade asked.

"During the past three months," Calder answered. "Incidentally, Lanham took over the Potter Mays holding about four months back."

"Now you're intimating, with no evidence, I gather, that Lanham has been mixed up in something off-color," Slade reproved.

The sheriff shrugged again. "Reckon you'd use one of your highfalutin' words to describe it. Coincidence, ain't it?" he said.

Slade smiled. "I guess it does apply, to an extent," he admitted. "Well, I'm going over to the hotel and register for a room. Want to shave and freshen up a bit. Then I think I'll walk across the bridge to Matamoros—my horse has done enough leg stretching for today—and have a talk with Amado Menendez."

"Don't you figure I'd better go along, just in case?" Calder suggested.

"Really I don't think there is any need for you to do so," Slade vetoed the notion. "And I feel it's best that you stick around here for a spell, against the chance that Charge Grundy and his bunch should show up. It's early, and I recall they were in a habit of coming to town the latter part of the week."

"Guess you're right there," the sheriff conceded. "If they show up and try to start something with the Bar L bunch, I'll bear down on

’em proper. Okay, see you tomorrow. That is if you don’t manage to get mixed up in something tonight—wouldn’t put it past you.”

Slade laughed and stood up. He glanced toward where Dixon Lanham and his men were drinking at the bar. The Bar L owner caught his eye and waved. Slade waved back. As he sauntered to the door, he noted that Lanham and his bunch had drawn heads together, their eyes glinting in his direction. Which, circumstances being what they were, was not too surprising, Slade reasoned. Very likely had been the subject of discussion during the course of the evening—discussion Sheriff Calder would have been dubious about. For the stubborn old peace officer was “set in his ways” and like the chick with the piece of egg shell on its back, largely believed only what he could see, and was sometimes doubtful about even that.

Pausing at Shadow’s stable, Slade retrieved his saddle pouches and made his way to the nearby hotel, where he registered for a room in which he stowed the pouches. He shaved, bathed, donned clean shirt and overalls and, fairly well satisfied with the general result, headed for Matamoros, taking his time about it and looking the town over as he walked.

Brownsville was, as usual, busy and bustling. The streets were crowded. All the saloons were enjoying plenty of patronage, as were the shops.

For the little city was prosperous and becoming more so as time went on despite the depredations of outlaws and cow thieves and the frequent turmoil south of the river.

As he neared the approaches of the bridge at the foot of Fourteenth Street, he smiled as he glanced in the direction of the Last Chance saloon run by one Burley Sturm whom the sheriff had regarded sideways until Sturm had proved himself. Later, Sturm had married Teresa, Dolores Malone's youthful aunt, and Amado Menendez' sister. She had inherited the famed beauty of the Menendez women, as had her niece, and she also had inherited from somewhere an impish sense of humor that could be devastating, as Slade had good cause to remember.

Without incident, Slade crossed the bridge and reached Matamoros, a city of sunbaked adobe and stone, a typical Mexican Border town with sleepy plazas, and a ragged edge of squalid pole and mud huts hemming them in. It had been burned twice and pillaged more than once.

Life centered around the Plaza de Hidalgo, which was surrounded by the better homes and the buildings of the civil and federal governments, and by a huddle of curio shops, miniature bazaars, and saloons. Outward from the plaza were low, one-story structures, mostly of brick, built close against the narrow sidewalks.

Slade liked Matamoros, which was always gay

and colorful, despite the fact that many of its inhabitants had little to be gay about. He took his time, sauntering through the plaza, pausing from time to time to gaze at the curious goods displayed in the various stalls. Finally he headed for La Luz, Amado Menendez' cantina, by way of a poorly lighted and, at this time of night, little frequented street faced by blank-windowed closed shops and warehouses.

He was not far from the corner where he would turn toward the cantina, when he saw a man approaching from the opposite direction. He walked with his head slung forward and his gait was a bit unsteady. No doubt, he had been celebrating a mite too much. The fellow lurched past a dark alley mouth, where abruptly there was a blur of movement. Another instant and he flung up his head and screamed—a horrible, agonized scream that crescendoed into a blood-bubbling shriek. Then he plunged forward on his face.

Slade halted, then bounded forward, and went sideways against the building wall as again he sensed movement in the alley mouth.

A gun blazed from the darkness, a bullet fanned his face. A second just touched the brim of his hat. He whipped out both Colts and sprayed the alley mouth with lead.

A cry of pain echoed with the gun reports, and a thudding of fast feet. Slade hesitated a moment, then glided forward, guns ready for instant action. Cautiously, he peered into the alley and saw two men just rounding the corner at the far end, one undoubtedly limping.

Pursuit would be useless, for the pair could lose themselves in any of the narrow and crooked streets. He turned back from the alley.

And for the second time that day, Walt Slade looked upon a dead man!

3

The victim, short and stocky of build, was dressed in rangeland clothes. Between his shoulder blades protruded the haft of a long knife.

Shouts were now sounding in the distance; evidently the shooting had been heard. Slade turned the body over, gazed into the face dimly outlined by the feeble beams of a street light. He did not recall having seen it before.

The shouts were drawing nearer. He glided into the alley and swiftly reached the far end, turned a corner, and another, then, at a leisurely pace, continued on his way to La Luz. Reaching the cantina, he strolled in.

As usual, La Luz was crowded, and everybody appeared to be having a good time. The lighting was soft without being gloomy. The furnishings were of excellent quality and in good taste. A really good orchestra played dreamy music.

Big, portly, jovial Amado Menendez was standing at the far end of the bar conversing with a girl in the short spangled skirt and low-cut bodice of the dance floor. She was not very big, but her figure left nothing to be desired. She had curly black hair, plenty of it, astonishingly big and darkly blue eyes, startlingly red lips, and a creamily tanned complexion. Altogether, calculated to arouse masculine interest, and hold it.

Such was Dolores Malone, Texas born, daughter of Terence Malone, an Irish adventurer and soldier of fortune. Charming, likeable, as was usual with his kind, he had married one of the beautiful Menendez women, Amado Menendez' older sister, but had not been overly successful in a financial way. So when he died, less than a year after his wife had passed on, Dolores went to work dancing in her uncle's cantina. Amado would have gladly supported her, but Dolores held that a Texas girl capable of supporting herself should not be dependent on relatives.

She was indeed, very quickly, much more than a dance floor girl, running La Luz in Amado's absence and, it was rumored, largely in his presence.

Amado glanced toward the door, stared, let out a whoop that shook the rafters. He came bounding across the room for, big as he was, he was like a cat on his feet; but Dolores outdistanced him with ease and fairly flung herself into Slade's arms.

"So you came back to Dolores, and so soon!" she shrilled. "Did all the others tell you to *vamos*?"

"What others?" he demanded indignantly, holding her close. Dolores laughed gaily.

"It doesn't matter," she said. "You're here, and that's all that counts!"

Amado enveloped them both with his long arms, in a bear hug.

"Wine!" he bellowed in a tone that sent half a dozen waiters scurrying. "The golden wine that Amado drinks! For this is a day! *Capitán*, it is grand to see you once again! Come, come and sit, and we drink to past days, and days to come!"

He led the way to a table near the dance floor. A waiter was instantly beside them, a bottle under each arm, crystal tumblers in his hands, which he filled to the brim with wine that was distilled sunshine.

"Well, a wonderful welcome," Slade said. "How are you, Amado? It's fine to see *you* again."

"How about me?" Dolores pouted. "Isn't it fine to see me again, too?"

"Such a vision of loveliness leaves one speechless," he replied.

"Hmmm! So somebody has taught you to say pretty things," she said. "Be careful, a neglected woman has been known to retaliate."

"Or—cooperate," he smiled.

Dolores giggled, and didn't press the point.

Amado raised his glass in salute.

"To *El Halcón,* the good, the just," he said softly. Slade bowed his acknowledgment of the toast and they drank.

Abruptly Slade's attention was distracted from his companions. Six men had just entered the cantina. They were Dixon Lanham and his five hands. Slade's black brows drew together as he noticed that one walked with a slight limp.

Not that there was anything so unusual about a cow puncher limping. Handling stock was a rough occupation and accidents often happened. But it *was* interesting.

Lanham paused just inside the swinging doors and swept the room with his pale glance. He spotted Slade and waved his hand. Slade waved a reply to the greeting. And so did Amado.

"You know the Señor Lanham?" he asked of Slade.

"Met him this afternoon," the Ranger replied and did not detail the nature of the meeting, for the moment.

"Here he comes often," said Amado. "The good spender and himself and his hombres behave well, although I have heard that north of the river they sometimes do not. He likes the girls, especially my small niece."

"Is always a perfect gentleman on the floor," Dolores said. "I think," she added thoughtfully, "that he is a very lonely man."

This Slade also found to be of interest.

Lanham and his men made their way to the bar and ordered drinks, and began talking together, apparently paying no further attention to the occupants of the table near the dance floor.

At that juncture a pleasant-faced, elderly Mexican gentleman sauntered in, glanced around expectantly. Amado at once called him to join them.

It was the *Jefe Politico*, the Matamoros Chief of Police. He and Slade were old *amigos* and had a warm greeting for each other.

The chief sat down, accepted a glass of wine and twinkled his shrewd old eyes at Slade. *El Halcón* had a pretty good notion as to just what he had on his mind.

"To the back room go I, from whence stock is needed," Amado announced. "You, *Capitán*, see I will later."

"And to the dance floor go I," mimicked Dolores as her uncle bounced off. "For there needed I am. Lots of business tonight. *You,* darling, see *I* will later." She trotted to the floor and a little later was dancing with Dixon Lanham. Slade regarded the chief expectantly.

"*Capitán,*" the chief said, "tonight on a Matamoros street a man died."

"With a knife in his back," Slade supplied. The chief did not appear surprised.

"You saw it done?" he asked.

"I saw what little there was to see," Slade replied. "It happened in the matter of a split second. I would say the devils were waiting in the alley for him to pass. One darted out and knifed him. They threw a little lead at me, but it didn't connect."

"So I can see," the chief said dryly. "Did you—connect, *Capitán*?"

"Pretty sure I nicked one in the leg," Slade answered. "He was limping when he rounded the corner from the alley."

"I see," the chief nodded. "*Capitán*, tonight makes three in less than a month, all *Americanos*."

"Looks like you might have a feud of some sort on your hands," Slade commented.

"*Capitán*, I know not," the chief replied. "But there is anger north of the river, and what happened tonight will serve to fan the embers. Relations between the two cities are beginning to become strained, which is most unfortunate."

"Yes, very unfortunate," Slade agreed. He was silent for a few minutes, his eyes thoughtful, the chief watching him expectantly. Finally he spoke, "Is there by chance another *libertador*, so called, poking up his head from the bushes?"

"*Capitán*," said the chief, "again I know not. All I can say is there are whispers, as always. Whispers of a rising against the government of *El Presidente*, with vengeance upon those north of the river who have wronged the people of *Mejico*."

"I see," Slade said. "Very likely another outlaw leader out to try and make hay in sunshine or shadow, caring not what happens to the misguided who listen to his perverted counsel. Same old story. That which has plagued Brownsville and Matamoros time and again. Well, our chore is to find out who is the big he-wolf of the pack and eliminate him."

"Which *Capitán* will do," the chief declared confidently.

"Hope so," Slade said. "Any notion whom he might be?"

"Sadly I must confess I have not," the chief replied.

"Were the two men recently killed cowhands?" Slade continued.

"So they appeared," answered the chief.

"Did any spread north of the river claim them as riders?"

"I understand, no," said the chief.

"Which tends to support our theory that an outlaw bunch, very likely from some other area, Texas or elsewhere, is working the section," Slade said thoughtfully.

"So I would presume," the chief conceded.

"Yes, the same old story, following a familiar pattern ever since the days of Cheno Cortinas, who actually once captured Brownsville and held the city for forty-eight hours, looting and killing. I rather doubt any enterprising gent will be able to duplicate Cortinas' feat, but you never can tell for sure, should he get together enough of a following south of the Rio Grande. Well, we'll see."

"*Capitán*," said the chief, "do you think that by any chance those two killers tonight were also lying in wait for you?"

"Does it seem logical to think so?" Slade countered. "So far as I am aware, nobody over here knew I planned to visit Matamoros."

"But could not someone north of the river have anticipated your intention and preceded you here?"

"It is possible," Slade was forced to admit.

The old chief apparently had a shrewd mind. He regarded *El Halcón* for a moment, then remarked, "Does not it seem strange that those killers would have paused to shoot at you instead of fleeing the instant they accomplished their apparent purpose, the slaying of that unfortunate?"

Again Slade had to admit the chief might have something there. He glanced thoughtfully at the bar, his eyes focusing for a moment on a group there. The chief sipped his wine and drew forth an old black pipe which he stuffed with even blacker tobacco. He twinkled his eyes at Slade.

"*Ai*!" he said, "life brings many a trial; who is without them? But *Capitán* has dispatched many a *ladron* who posed as a *libertador* but was only a Border *bandido*, and rid the world of the snakes that followed him. History will itself repeat."

"*Gracias* for your confidence," Slade smiled.

Amado joined them and indulged in a glass of

wine. Dolores trotted over from the dance floor and plumped herself into a chair.

"Darling," she said to Slade, "you must dance the next number with me. It is a waltz, and you love waltzes."

It *was* a waltz, an immortal composition by the Waltz King of Vienna. The chief enthused as they glided onto the floor together, "The splendid couple they make! She a *señorita* most beautiful! He a magnificent man!"

4

The chief was not guilty of overstatement. Walt Slade was very tall, more than six feet, and the breadth of his shoulders and the depth of his chest were commensurate with his height.

His face was as arresting as his form. A rather wide mouth, grin-quirked at the corners, somewhat relieved the tinge of fierceness evinced by the prominent hawk nose above and the powerful jaw and chin beneath. His broad forehead was surmounted by thick, crisp hair so black that in certain lights a blue shadow seemed to lie upon it.

The sternly handsome countenance was dominated by long, black-lashed eyes of a very pale gray. Cold, reckless eyes that nevertheless always seemed to have little gay devils of laughter lurking in their clear depths. Devils that could be anything but laughing when they leaped to the front—if occasion warranted. Then the eyes became "the terrible eyes of *El Halcón*," which would give armed men pause.

Slade wore, with careless grace, the homely, efficient garb of the rangeland—bibless overalls, soft blue shirt with vivid neckerchief looped at the throat, half-boots of softly tanned leather, and the broad-brimmed "J.B.," the rainshed of the plains.

Around his sinewy waist were double cartridge

belts, from the carefully oiled and worked cut-out holsters of which protruded the plain black butts of heavy guns. And from the butts of those big Colts, his slender, muscular hands seemed never far away.

Slade danced two numbers with Dolores, then rejoined Amado and the chief. Dolores remained on the floor, for now business was really good, with plenty of gentlemen desiring dances.

"Ha!" Amado suddenly exclaimed, "enters, the fine gentleman."

Slade had already noticed the tall and very handsome man who had just strolled in. His shoulders were broad, his lines long and lean. He had dark hair with just a sprinkling of gray and dark eyes. Keen looking eyes, Slade thought, that doubtless missed little. He waved a greeting to Amado and turned toward the bar.

"Who is he?" *El Halcón* asked.

"It is the Señor Alden Drake," the cantina owner replied. "He is a lawyer and he buys and sells land. In Brownsville he lives, but he likes Matamoros and here comes often. He has obtained justice in the courts for several Texas Mexicans, and hopes to, in the future, be able to practice his profession in Matamoros. Always is he courteous and considerate, especially to the girls and the help, even as is *Capitán*."

"Sounds interesting," Slade said. "I don't recall seeing him when I was here before."

"Only the four months and the week or two has he been here," said Amado. "He came not long after *Capitán* was here last."

Slade noted that Drake had found a place at the bar next to the Bar L bunch and was conversing with Dixon Lanham. Then he forgot all about him, for another newcomer had just pushed through the swinging doors.

He was a tall young Yaqui Mexican with a dark, savage face and piercing black eyes, whose height denoted more than a little Spanish blood.

It was one Estevan, with whom Slade had shared stirring adventures, a most loyal friend and a strong stick to lean on in time of difficulty or trouble. His teeth flashed white in a smile as he made his way to the table, seeming to glide rather than walk. Slade arose to meet him and shake hands, and wave him to the chair Dolores had vacated.

"How are you, Estevan?" he said. "Good to see you again."

"And most good it is to see you again, *Capitán*," the Mexican returned. "Ha! Now will the business pick up, as you would say."

Amado and Slade both chuckled as the former poured a glass of wine. Estevan was never happy unless there was trouble brewing.

"Is *Capitán* the trail on?" he asked hopefully.

"In a way, I guess, although I hardly know what trail or where it is heading," Slade replied.

"*Capitán* will learn, and know," Estevan said complacently. "I and my *amigos* will the watch keep that we may be of help."

"You were certainly a great help more than once and more than twice in the past," Slade assured him. Estevan bowed low.

"To the help be to *El Halcón*, the good, the just, is the honor great," he murmured.

Dolores came bouncing over to greet Estevan, who was a prime favorite with her and the other girls, although Slade privately believed women were the only creatures Estevan was ever afraid of.

"A man they do affright, for of surprises full are they," he was wont to declare.

"Just the same, he *looks,*" Dolores said, with a giggle.

Estevan lingered for a short time, over a second glass of wine, then departed to, Slade knew, "the watch keep," and listen.

A little later, the chief also sauntered out. Amado returned to the end of the bar, and with Dolores still on his dance floor, Slade was left alone to his cigarette and his thoughts.

The cigarette, aided and abetted by a cup of steaming coffee, was satisfactory; the thoughts were not. No doubt but that trouble of some sort was building up along the river, trouble that could spill over into Texas, bringing turmoil and bloodshed unless thwarted in time. And he felt it was up to him to do the "thwarting," as he had once before.

Slade knew the land south of the Rio Grande was cruelly misgoverned, the ruling powers, spearheaded by old El Presidente Porfirio Diaz, subscribing to the principle that the rich should grow richer, the poor poorer. The unfortunate land policies of Diaz resulted in more than ten-million persons losing prescriptive rights to the previously inalienable communal lands of the free villages and becoming *peónes* on the great *haciendas* which absorbed the erstwhile village lands. In short, the masses were in a state of greater degradation than ever before. Under such conditions, a great socio-economic upheaval was ultimately inevitable.

And from it would rise a new Mexico, free and prosperous, that would stand shoulder to shoulder with America in an hour of mutual trial.

Yes, it would come, but not yet; the time was not ripe. And meanwhile the unscrupulous, with only their own greedy ends in view, would lead their ignorant and superstitious dupes to the slaughter.

Alden Drake, Slade noted, was leaving. Dixon Lanham, after conversing with his hands for a little while, began making his way slowly to the dance floor, diagonalling from the bar.

Across the room from where Slade sat, but not directly in line with his table, was the black square of a window that opened into an alley, a window that Slade, as a matter of habit, kept an eye on, as he did on the swinging doors.

Suddenly he leaped to his feet, hands streaking to his holsters. In the darkness beyond the window he had sensed movement, and his amazingly keen eyes had seen the shadowy outline of a gun thrusting forward across the sill.

Slade drew and shot a split second before that shadowy gun spurted fire. The bullet from it thudded into the ceiling as it flew sideways from the hand that held it. From the darkness came a yelp of pain, followed by the thud of running steps.

Skirting tables, chairs, and people by miracles of agility, Slade charged across the room to the window, went through it feet first in a streaking dive. He struck the ground solidly but kept his balance, weaving and ducking, his cocked gun thrusting forward.

But a single swift glance through the gloom told him there was nobody in the alley. However, there were openings between the various buildings that flanked it, into any of which the drygulcher could have darted.

On the chance that his slug had done more than superficial damage, he glided to several of the nearer openings. He peered in, but found nothing. Turning, he made his way back to the cantina, which stood near the corner, and which at the moment was a fair sample of bedlam on a busy day. Yells, curses, the shrieks of the dance floor girls filled the air.

Amado Menendez leaned out the window, spewing profanity in three languages and holding up a bracket lamp.

At the same instant, the back door of the cantina banged open and two figures shot out like pits squeezed from an orange. One was Dolores Malone, and she held a cocked gun in her hand. The other was Estevan, swinging a long throwing knife back and forth by the point.

"All is well, *Capitán*?" he called anxiously.

"No complaint," Slade replied as he walked to meet them.

Dolores ran to him. "Oh, darling!" she panted. "Did they try to kill you?"

"They tried to kill somebody," Slade answered grimly.

Although he did not choose to mention it at the moment, he knew very well the slug had not been intended for himself.

That dimly seen gun had been trained on the back of Dixon Lanham!

5

Slade and his companions reached the door before anybody else could come out. This was not strange. Standing on either side of this door, facing another door that led to the barroom, was a dark-faced young Yaqui Mexican swinging a throwing knife by the point. They were two of Estevan's *amigos* making sure nobody attacked their chief from the rear.

As Slade well knew, Estevan and his followers worked with the precision of a well oiled and perfectly coordinated machine. He smiled and nodded to them. Both bowed low and sheathed their knives as Estevan closed and locked the back door.

"And it might be a good idea for you to put the hammer down on that thing," Slade said to Dolores, gesturing to the big gun in her hand, that was still at full cock.

"Wanted to be sure I wouldn't need it before I did," she replied as she obeyed and dropped the forty-five in a drawer.

In the barroom, Slade was bombarded with questions, which he tried to answer briefly.

"I just saw a gun thrust through the window and was afraid it might go off and hurt somebody," he explained at one point.

A roar of laughter greeted the remark, which

relieved the tension, and the place began to quiet down.

"How did you get here so fast?" he asked of Estevan as they moved to their table, Dolores clinging to Slade's arm.

"In the door I was just coming when *Capitán* the room crossed like a shadow before a cloud," Estevan replied. "*La señorita* was to the back room flying. I followed."

"*Gracias*," Slade replied.

"It was the pleasure great," the Mexican answered. "Only regret I there was no use for my blade; it is thirsty. Regret I, too, that the *ladrón* escaped."

"So do I," Slade said. "But I think he will have a sore hand by which to remember me."

"*Bueno*!" said Estevan.

Dixon Lanham approached the Ranger. "Mr. Slade," he said, "do you always do things like that? And do you ever miss?"

"The light was good," Slade deprecated the feat.

"That's right," Lanham agreed dryly. "About as good as at the bottom of a well at midnight."

With a shake of his head, he turned to the bar. Slade's eyes followed him for a moment, and they were intensely speculative. Dixon Lanham was suddenly very much of an enigma. *Why* had somebody deliberately tried to murder him?

Evidently word of the happening had quickly gotten around, for the cantina, which was well crowded before, was now jam packed with people excitedly discussing the incident. Slade was favored with admiring glances. But Amado and his floor men shooed away the curious. Estevan's dark glare was also a deterrent.

An exception was made when Alden Drake, the lawyer and land speculator, hurried in, swept the room with his keen eyes, and then approached Amado and Dixon Lanham, who were standing together at the bar. Several moments of talk followed, which Slade could not quite catch. Then Drake was led to his table.

"Mr. Slade," Lanham said, "I'd like you to know Mr. Alden Drake, of whom Amado spoke. Mr. Drake, I guess an introduction is hardly needed, but this is Mr. Slade, Sheriff Calder's deputy."

"Glad and honored to know you, Mr. Slade," Drake said as they shook hands, his grip firm but not unpleasantly so. "I gather that you saved somebody from being killed. I wonder who that scoundrel had in mind."

"Hard to tell," the Ranger replied. "He'd just shoved the gun forward when I spotted him."

"And shot it from his hand!" Drake said, shaking his head in admiration.

Slade repeated his former statement, "The light was good."

Both his hearers laughed politely and did not appear much impressed.

"Anyhow, it was an admirable piece of work,"

Drake said. "Well, hope to see you again, Mr. Slade. I was just going for my horse when I heard the shooting in this direction and thought I'd investigate. Now I'll make another try at getting across the river and to bed."

With a smile and a nod he departed, his eyes again sweeping the room, centering in frank admiration on Dolores.

"A really the very nice *hombre*," said Amado.

Lanham bobbed his head in agreement, and went back to his men at the bar. A moment later, Estevan smiled at Slade and also drifted out.

"And I'm going to change," Dolores said. "I've had enough of this for one night. Besides, the flowers and the little house on Jackson Street are lonely."

She slanted a glance at Slade through her lashes and scampered off to the dressing room.

While Slade was awaiting her return, the *Jefe Politico* strolled in, sat down and regarded Slade.

"Understand *Capitán* has been a busy *hombre*," he remarked suggestively.

Feeling that he should know, Slade recounted the incident in detail, including his conviction that Dixon Lanham had been the drygulcher's target. The chief gazed at the Bar L owner for a moment. "Men make enemies," he said.

"And sometimes men are in somebody's way," Slade replied.

"That too is so," the chief conceded. "I wonder in whose way the Señor Lanham might be?"

"A question to which I'd very much like to have the answer," *El Halcón* returned soberly.

"*Capitán* will it get," the chief said, with conviction. "Him I will see again. Now my couch I seek; old bones need rest."

Dolores reappeared, very charming, Slade thought, in her riding costume of Levi's and soft blue shirt, well open at the throat.

"I'll walk beside your horse," he told her.

"You'll do nothing of the sort," she stated flatly. "You will walk beside *me*. The horse is all right where he is; I'll pick him up tomorrow. Walking is good for my figure."

"Been doing a lot of it recently, eh?" he remarked, with an all-embracing glance.

"Another pretty thing to say that you learned in the course of your absence," she replied. "Well, I can stand a few compliments."

"I would imagine you are surfeited with them," he replied.

"But the value of a compliment is enhanced by the source from whence it comes," she said softly. "Let's go, dear."

Slade paid little attention to his surroundings as they walked across the bridge and through Brownsville's quiet streets; he knew that he and Dolores were well "chaperoned." For behind and in front, unseen, unheard, but grimly real were Estevan and his Yaqui knife men with eyes that missed nothing, their long blades thirsty.

Early the following afternoon, Slade met with Sheriff Calder in the latter's office, and gave him a detailed account of his experience in La Luz, mentioning also his meeting with Alden Drake, the lawyer and land speculator.

" 'Pears to be all right," Calder said, apropos of Drake. "Came here, well recommended, from Dallas. Smart, all right; has made a couple of shrewd land deals and won some cases. Wonder what he and Dixon Lanham had to discuss?"

"I can think of a possible explanation," Slade replied. "He told me Charge Grundy claims a portion of his land, the real basis of trouble between them. After I scolded him for taking the law into his own hands, he may have decided to seek recourse in the courts, probably surmising that after I talked to Grundy, Charge might go to court and bring suit. He may have retained Drake to handle the matter."

"Yep, that could be it," Calder agreed. "Well, he could do worse; Drake is no snide when it comes to such business. By the way, I saw Lanham and his young hellions leave the Blue Bell, but thought they were headed home," he continued. "If I'd knowed they figured to cross the river I'd have been right after them. You sure that drygulcher didn't intend to line sights with you instead of Lanham?"

"I am sure," Slade answered, "so don't go insinuating."

"Okay," grunted Calder. "Anyhow I won't in—in—what you call it out loud. Of course I know darn well, too, that some sidewinder who has recognized you as *El Halcón* may be out to settle a score. Plenty hereabouts that would be glad to do just that. That blasted *El Halcón* business worries me, just like it worries Jim McNelty.

"Oh, I know, as *El Halcón* a lot of folks figure you to be just a blasted owlhoot too smart to get caught so far, and able to pull the wool over the eyes of some stupid sheriffs. Naturally, you get to hear and see things you wouldn't get to see and hear if it was generally knowed you are a Ranger. And the real owlhoots, figuring you're just one of their brand hornin' in on the good things they have started, sometimes get a mite careless, like they wouldn't do with a Ranger, and end with their toes up, peacefully waiting for the undertaker. But I'm always scairt some loco deputy or marshal may take a shot at you, though I reckon you'd just wing him, not wanting to kill a peace officer, and then explain things while he was recovering.

"And then there's always the chance some professional gunslinger will try to plug you in the back, hankering to be knowed as the feller who downed the fastest gunhand in the whole Southwest. But sneakin' up on you from behind, of course, is just like sneakin' up on a rabbit that can see all ways at once. But just the same it bothers me."

Because of his habit of working undercover whenever possible and not revealing his Ranger connections, Walt Slade had built up a singular dual reputation. Those who knew the truth declared he was not only the most fearless but also the most able of the illustrious body of law enforcement officers. Some, as the sheriff said, knew him only as *El Halcón* and believed that he was an outlaw. But others who also just knew him as *El Halcón* were his stanch defenders, maintaining that he always worked on the side of law and order, and that reputable peace officers like Sheriff Calder were glad to have his help when the going got rough.

And, what Slade values most of all, was that the *peónes* and other humble folk would say, "*El Halcón*! the good, the just, the compassionate, the friend of the lowly! May *El Dios* ever guard him!"

So Slade went his carefree way as *El Halcón*, and worried about what might happen in consequence not at all.

"And now what?" asked the sheriff.

"I'll be darned if I know," Slade replied. "We appear to be getting exactly nowhere. Two mysterious killings and an equally mysterious attempt at a killing in a twenty-four-hour period. Hints of a Border rising, with plenty of indications of trouble of one sort or another along the river. And somewhere in the background an elusive and sinister mastermind pulling the wires. And no definite suspect, so far as I can see. Now you go ahead and do some guessing."

The sheriff's reaction was an explosive snort and an accusing glare. "Let me get a notion and you go right ahead and whack it down," he said in an injured voice.

"A notion without something definite on which to base it is of little value," Slade pointed out.

The sheriff growled. "Oh, the devil!" he grumbled. "I'll fetch us some coffee; maybe that'll help get the think tank going."

Slade laughed, and did not object, accepting the steaming cup with a smile. Calder drew a black bottle from a drawer and spiked his. Slade took his straight.

After the cups were empty, Slade announced, "I'm going to take a walk, maybe that will help."

"Watch your step," warned Calder. "No telling what is liable to cut loose in this hell-town, and I've a notion, with plenty on which to base it, that you ain't overly popular in certain quarters about now."

"I'll risk it," Slade said carelessly and walked out into the sunshine.

6

For some time, Slade wandered aimlessly around the town, stopping at several places, studying faces, listening to talk. He paused to gaze at the classic design of the ancient Miller Hotel on S. E. Elizabeth Street. It had been the social center of early Brownsville and had boasted as guests, among other personages, such noted generals as Ulysses S. Grant, Robert E. Lee, Zachary Taylor, and Philip H. Sheridan.

Now, Slade thought, it had a forlorn look as it basked in the pale, shadowy sunshine of departed greatness. He continued his stroll.

Gradually, he worked his way to Fourteenth Street, near the bridge, and smiled as he entered the Last Chance.

Standing at the far end of the bar was big, rugged Burley Sturm, and beside him was a very beautiful young lady. She was Teresa, his wife and Dolores Malone's aunt. The lady gave a glad little cry and ran to greet him, holding out both sun-golden hands, over which Slade bowed with courtly grace.

"Dolores stopped on her way to work and told us you were here," she chattered. "We were hoping you'd drop in. Come, sit down and have a drink with us, and tell us all about what you've been doing while you were away. Dolores looked positively radiant, and I don't wonder!"

Sturm, bobbing and grinning, also came forward. He and Slade shook hands warmly. They occupied a table. A waiter came hurrying with glasses and bottles.

For some time they talked over their drinks, Slade briefly recounting his experiences during the past few months.

"He makes it sound so prosaic and commonplace," Teresa complained. "We'll never get the true story. Oh, well, it doesn't matter. All that really matters, Walt, is that were it not for you, Burley and I would not have attained the happiness with which we are blessed."

Sturm, gazing fondly at his pretty wife, voiced emphatic agreement.

"I think you would have anyway," Slade replied. "You were meant for each other."

"Um-huh," said Sturm, "but it took *El Halcón* to make us realize it. Expect to be here long this time, Walt?"

"It looks a little that way," the Ranger replied.

"What I wish most of all is that you'd make it for good, and I'm not alone in wishing," Teresa said. "Oh I know, the lure of the trail is greater than that of any woman."

But she smiled a little sadly as she apparently understood the familiar longing in his soul, the yearning toward far horizons that seemed to whisper to the lonely horseman, "Come and see!"

Finally Slade glanced at the clock over the back bar, smiled at his companions and said, "Well, guess I'd better be getting back to the sheriff's office to learn if there's anything new. I'll be seeing you both again soon."

In silence they watched him pass out into the glory of the sunset, pause for a moment to gaze westward.

"Always he looks into the sunset," Teresa murmured.

"And beyond," Sturm said.

Farther along the street, from where he had a better view, Slade again paused to gaze toward that flaming splendor of many hues. Then through the gathering dusk he made his way to the sheriff's office, where he found Calder smoking his pipe and waiting.

"Well, learn anything?" he asked.

"Nothing," Slade replied. "But Estevan and his *amigos* are browsing about on both sides of the river and may have something to tell us, later."

"Wouldn't be surprised," agreed the sheriff. "Those young hellions don't miss much."

He fetched coffee from the back room and for a while they sat sipping it and smoking in silence, each busy with his own thoughts. Finally Calder glanced at the dark window.

"Guess we might as well amble over to the Blue Bell and tie onto a surrounding," he suggested.

"If Estevan should have something to tell us, he'll know he can find us there when the office is closed."

Slade was agreeable and they set out. Fats Boyer, the owner, led them to the table he always had in reserve and they sat down and put in their orders. They had just finished eating when Estevan glided in.

He did not approach the table, but found a place at the bar and ordered a drink. Boyer, who knew him well, was behind the bar at the moment and served him. They spoke together for a few minutes. Estevan did not glance toward Slade and the sheriff.

"He always works that way," Slade said. "Never makes things look obvious. He'll be turning in this direction shortly, as if he did not know we were here."

Slade was right. Estevan did finally deign to glance toward the table and nodded as if surprised.

"Come and have a drink with us," Slade called.

Estevan accepted the invitation and occupied a chair. For a little while, he sipped his wine in silence, his glittering black eyes slanting in every direction.

Slade waited, also in silence, for he and Estevan had something in common: neither would talk until ready to do so. Finally the knife man did speak, his voice low, his lips moving not at all.

"*Capitán*," he said, "in a cantina, what the *Señor* Sheriff would call a hole-of-the-rum, of repute not good, men five drank and talked. One of my *amigos* stood not off too far and listened. Much he could not hear, but something he did. 'He will meet,' said one of the men. Said another, 'A cinch.' Cinch means to put on the cayuse the saddle and bridle, does it not?"

"Yes, in cowhand talk," Slade replied. "But it also is slang for 'easy to accomplish.' "

"Ha! sense that makes," said Estevan. "Something they to do expect without difficulty."

"Very likely," Slade agreed. "Did your *amigo* hear anything else?"

"He heard one say, 'Los Indios.' "

"Los Indios," Slade repeated. "That is a little hamlet close to the river, about twenty miles to the northwest of here. Los Indios! What can the devils have in mind? No bank there. No stage station. Nothing that would appeal to an outlaw bunch."

"Remember the last time you were here we busted up a bunch of hellions who aimed to tie onto the money a storekeeper had stashed away to buy smuggled goods with," the sheriff put in. "Might be something like that."

"I doubt it," Slade answered. "There's no establishment in Los Indios similar to Arbuckle's stores. Smugglers don't operate there."

"Close by, though, there's a good ford by

way of which cows could be shoved across to Mexico," the sheriff reminded.

"Yes, they could have a little chore of cattle stealing in mind, which I understand has happened several times of late," Slade said. "That ford is not so very far west of Charge Grundy's holding."

"And right in line with Dixon Lanham's Bar L," the sheriff remarked significantly.

Slade looked at him but did not otherwise offer reproof. "What else, Estevan?" he asked.

"As dark fell the men left the cantina," Estevan replied. "My *amigo* said that one walked with a limp not slight."

"Hmmm!" interpolated the sheriff, again significantly.

This time Slade did not deign to spare him a look. "Did he learn where they headed for?" he asked of Estevan.

"They rode north and west on the Camino Real, the old royal road that from presidio to presidio ran in the days of the Spanish king, which is the travelled little at night," Estevan answered.

"Doubtless planning to ford the river farther on," Slade guessed. "That way they would attract less attention than by riding through Brownsville and west by way of the Laredo-Brownsville trail."

For several moments he sat silent, his black

brows drawing together, while his companions watched him expectantly.

"I think," he said at length, "that we'll take a little ride to Los Indios. They'd hardly pull anything before midnight, and we should make it there by then. Tom, I see Deputy Webley is at the bar. Tell him to round up your other deputy and meet us at the stable. Suppose you'd like to come along, Estevan?"

"*Si*," accepted the knife man, smiling broadly. "My *caballo* is at the rack outside. You will I join where Levee Street meets the trail."

Slade nodded agreement, knowing that such furtive moves appealed to the wild Yaqui blood that coursed through Estevan's veins. The knife man smiled again and eased out as unobtrusively as a shadow.

The sheriff went to the bar and spoke with Webley, a grizzled and sinewy old-timer, who nodded his understanding, finished his drink, and sauntered out in a leisurely manner, attracting no attention.

Slade and the sheriff waited a little longer, then also left. Once outside, they hurried to the stable and cinched up with speed.

The chore was barely finished, when Webley and the other deputy arrived, and a few minutes later the posse was riding the trail, Estevan, mounted on a rangy mustang that showed signs of speed and endurance, having joined them.

"I believe your *amigo* said the bunch in the cantina numbered five, and it was indicated that somebody else would meet them later, quite likely the head of the outfit, who preferred not to appear in Matamoros," Slade remarked to the knife man. "Which means that the odds are against us by one, maybe more. Well, with the element of surprise on our side we should make out, and with good luck bag the whole bunch. That is, if my hunch is a straight one and there's a little widelooping in the offing. Okay, let's go."

They rode on at a good pace. Shadow, who disliked being cooped up and thoroughly enjoyed such night rambles, wanted to really extend himself, but Slade curbed him in deference to his companions' slower mounts. From time to time he studied the back trail, a gray shimmer in the starlight, although he thought it unlikely they would be followed. Finally, satisfied they were not wearing a tail, he faced to the front and scanned the terrain ahead.

They passed Santa Rita, many years ago the headquarters of Cheno Cortinas, the Red Robber of the Rio Grande. Then La Paloma, named for a song, and continued on their way.

It lacked still some time till midnight as they neared Los Indios, for they had made really good progress without incident.

"Everything going plumb smooth, just like that

ride we took to Hidalgo months ago," the sheriff remarked.

"Yes, perhaps too darn smoothly," Slade replied. Because for no apparent reason, he was experiencing a premonition that all was not as it should be. He berated himself for an overactive imagination, but the feeling persisted, and was very disquieting. He scanned the north for any signs of approaching cattle, strained his ears to catch the slightest noise. But the prairie lay deserted, and no alien sound broke the great hush.

"Just a little farther on is the trail down to the ford," Calder said. "Going to ride down it?"

"We are not," Slade instantly said. "If somebody happened to be holed up in the brush down by the bank, we'd very likely be blown from under our hats. We pass Los Indios and keep on riding for half a mile or so. Then we'll circle around by way of the river bank, hole up the horses in the chaparral, and ease along through it until we are close to the ford. That way we should have everything under control, with the advantage ours even if the odds are against us."

"Makes sense," Calder admitted.

They passed Los Indios without incident. The little hamlet was to all appearances sound asleep, with no indications of disturbance of any kind. Once again Slade studied the back trail, and the rangeland to the north, and was somewhat encouraged by the utter silence and lack of movement. Began to look as if they were ahead of the possible wideloopers. A little farther, and he pulled to a halt.

"This should do it," he said. "The ford is quite a bit west of the town, and besides the folks that live there aren't much on mixing into matters they figure don't concern them. If they happen to hear some cows ambling this way from the north, they're very apt to shut their ears and go back to sleep. Okay, down to the river bank."

The maneuver was accomplished without difficulty. Close to the outer fringe of growth, they drifted the horses along toward the ford.

Again Slade called a halt. "Here we hole up the critters and hope they won't take a notion to sing songs to the stars at just the wrong time. Don't raise your voices above a whisper from now on; sounds travel a long way on a night like this," he warned.

He dropped the split reins to the ground. The others tethered their mounts in the fringe of growth. Then the little posse stole forward on foot.

For the third time *El Halcón* signalled to halt. "This should be about right," he breathed. "Easy six-gun range. Now all we can do is wait."

Here the channel of deeper water ran close to the north bank. When the river was very low, the steamers plying between Laredo and Brownsville could not make it across the ledge, but with the stream at normal, as it was at the moment, the old flat-bottoms had no difficulty negotiating the passage. And the channel water was also not too deep to prevent cattle from crossing the channel, and then following the ledge that edged the ford and made the rest of the passage to Mexico easy.

Slade leaned forward a little, his gaze fixed on the black water hurrying past.

"See something?" whispered the sheriff.

"Yes," the Ranger answered. "Looks like a post sticking up a couple of feet from the ledge, just the other side of the channel."

"Maybe put there to mark the channel for the steamer pilots," the sheriff hazarded.

"Could be," Slade conceded, and turned his attention elsewhere, his ears attuned to catch the slightest sound coming from the north.

7

The wait that followed was tedious, and slightly nerve-wracking, with nobody knowing for sure just what to expect. It seemed to *El Halcón* that if a widelooped herd was being driven to the river, it certainly should have already put in an appearance. And the premonition that something was not as it should be steadily strengthened.

At last, something did happen. Nothing particularly surprising, however. At a bend of the river, about a mile to the west, birthed a glow, a sparkle, resolving into the rather feeble beam of a steamer's searchlight. There were still quite a few of them on the river.

"Well, there'll be no cows driven down to the ford until that thing passes," Slade whispered. "Move back a little, don't want that light falling on us."

On came the old scow, chug-chugging cheerfully, her paddles slapping the water, members of her crew moving about the lighted deck. She passed the posse, hugging the bank, close to where the trail came down to the ford.

A blinding yellowish glare! The muffled boom of an explosion! Displaced air screeched past the posse that stood paralyzed with astonishment.

The steamer rocked and swayed, a whole section of her bow torn away by the blast, water pouring through the gaping hole.

The crew yelled and cursed. The pilot frantically spun the spokes of his wheel, endeavoring to beach the wrecked craft before it sank in the deeper water of the channel.

The steamer grounded. And from the growth just beyond the ford bulged half a dozen masked men, shooting as they came. The pilot screamed with pain and dropped beside his wheel.

"Let them have it!" Slade roared and drew and shot with both hands.

Followed a corpse and cartridge session for fair. The outlaws, taken as utterly by surprise as had been the steamer's crew, nevertheless fought back viciously, trading shots with the posse, firing at the flashes. One owlhoot was down, but the remaining five blazed away as fast as they could squeeze triggers. But they were in the light, the posse in the shadow of the growth.

Back and forth gushed the lances of flame, streaking through the gloom. Slade shot right and left and a second man fell. The posse guns boomed a volley and a third raider was accounted for.

Of the three left on their feet, one was a tall, broad-shouldered man. Slade lined sights with him, but at that instant another lurched in front of him, caught the slug and went down without a sound. The tall man shouted an order. He and his remaining companion whirled and dived into the brush, lead screaming after them.

Slade bounded forward, but before he reached the ford there was a crashing in the growth and a beat of departing hoofs. He pulled up, gave his attention to the four on the ground, quickly decided there was nothing more to fear from them, and turned back to see how his companions had fared. He could hear Deputy Webley cursing fluently.

"Did you stop one?" Slade asked anxiously.

"Slug grazed my leg, nothing to bother about," the deputy replied. "But I'm scairt that poor devil of a pilot is bad hurt, from the way he yelped."

The steamer was pandemonium personified. Slade's great voice rolled through the tumult, stilling it. "Where's the captain?" he shouted.

"Here I am," that official replied, leaning over the tilted rail.

"Lower your gangplank so we can come aboard," Slade told him.

The captain hesitated, gazing somewhat askance at the tall Ranger.

"Dadblast it! This is the Law talking!" bawled the sheriff. "Do as he says."

The skipper evidently caught the gleam of the sheriff's badge for he gave the necessary orders. Slade hurried up the gangplank as soon as it was in place and entered the wheel house, where the pilot lay on the floor, moaning and muttering, a couple of the crew hovering over him.

A swift examination showed an ugly bullet tear through the fleshy part of his upper arm. It was bleeding freely.

Slade stepped out of the wheel house and whistled a loud, clear note. A few moments and Shadow came trotting to him, snorting inquiringly. Slade secured his medicants from the saddle pouches and quickly had the wound padded and bandaged, the bleeding stopped.

"Feel better?" he asked as he rolled and lighted a cigarette and put it between the pilot's lips.

"A helluva sight better," he replied, puffing hard. "You a sawbones?"

"Nope," Slade answered and turned to Calder, who was peering at the smashed bow.

"How in blazes did they do it?" he asked.

"Very simple, and very clever," Slade replied. "With a little hindsight, I now understand the meaning of that post sticking up above the ledge and just beyond the channel."

"Yes?" the sheriff prompted wonderingly.

"Yes," the Ranger explained, "wedged it in a crevice, ran a line from it to a tree trunk on the bank. Suspended from the line was a bundle of dynamite well studded with percussion caps. The bow hit it and up it went. Lucky somebody wasn't killed."

The sheriff said several things, none of them

complimentary to the genius who evolved the scheme. "Sure hope one of those carcasses is his," he concluded.

"I'm afraid not," Slade replied. "I figure the tall one who got away is the he-wolf of the pack. Yes, a very, very clever piece of work. Sure had me fooled completely." He turned to the captain. "I feel I'm safe in saying you are packing quite a bit of money in your office, yes?" he said interrogatively. Again the skipper hesitated, but evidently reassured by the gaze of the steady eyes, nodded his head in the affirmative.

"Yes, a consignment to the Brownsville bank. We don't often carry anything like such a sum. Wasn't supposed to be noised about, but I guess somebody learned about it somehow."

"So one would presume," Slade said dryly.

"And thanks to you gentlemen, the devils didn't get it."

Slade beckoned Estevan to the front. "Here is the man who really deserves the credit," he said. "It was he learned those devils were headed for here and figured they were up to no good. My opinion was that they planned to run a few stolen cows across to Mexico by way of the ford. Never occurred to me that they had a steamer in mind."

The captain seized Estevan's hand and shook it warmly, much to the knife man's embarrassment.

"And I've a prime notion that more than the money was saved," the skipper said. "Wouldn't be surprised if a few lives were saved; they struck me as the sort not given to leaving witnesses."

"It is possible," Slade conceded soberly.

"And you all deserve plenty of credit for the way you handled the situation," added the skipper. "Four out of six taken care of. Not a bad percentage. Not bad at all. You are certainly to be commended."

Slade deftly changed the subject. "Suppose you fetch a lantern and we'll give those bodies a once-over," he suggested.

The captain did so. By its light, the masks were stripped off to reveal hard-lined countenances with nothing outstanding about them so far as Slade could ascertain. Sheriff Calder emptied the pockets, turning up a rather large sum of money but nothing else of significance. He divided the money into two portions, one of which he pocketed, slipping the other into Estevan's hand.

"Guess your *amigos* can stand a drink or two," he said.

The knife man grinned and didn't argue.

"Cowhands, all of them, wouldn't you say?" Calder remarked to Slade, jerking his head toward the bodies.

"Had been, at one time or another," the Ranger answered.

"Just as I expected," the sheriff observed pointedly.

Slade smiled and didn't argue. He insisted on

a look at Deputy Webley's injury. The deputy had been right; it was little more than a scrape. A smear of antiseptic ointment took care of it.

"I think you'll find four horses tethered back in the brush. Most unlikely the pair that got away loosed their own two horses before they hightailed," Slade told the deputies.

Which proved to be the case. The horses were led out with the bodies roped across the saddles.

"What about the brands?" Calder asked.

"Altered burns, good slick-iron work, means nothing," Slade replied. "Well, guess you might as well tie onto your own nags and we'll head for town; be daylight by the time we get there. Captain, put the pilot to bed and we'll send a wagon to fetch him to town. And we'll notify your company, so they can dispatch a crew to put your boat in shape."

"I'll stow him between the sheets right away," the skipper promised, adding grimly, "I've got a couple of rifles in my cabin and my mate and I will sit the rest of the night beside that safe with 'em ready for business."

Slade nodded approval, although he felt there was little chance the outlaws would make a second try for the money.

"Well, not such a bad night, after all," remarked the sheriff as they headed for Brownsville.

"Could have been better," Slade replied. "The brains of the outfit escaped."

"Just a matter of time till he gets his come-uppance," Calder predicted cheerfully. "Just a matter of time."

The sun was well up when they reached town. The horses were stabled, the chores cared for. Calder shooed out the curious that, early though it was, had gathered, and everybody went to bed.

8

A few hours past noon. Slade and the sheriff sat in the latter's office and regarded the blanketed forms on the floor.

"Nope, nobody who's took a look at the side-winders can remember seeing them before," Calder said in answer to a question. "I'm expecting some bartenders in a little later. Bar-keeps see everything and may have clapped eyes on those varmints. Reckon it don't mean much, anyhow."

"Not unless somebody might recall with whom they associated, which could possibly provide us with a lead," Slade said.

"With so much goin's and comin's in this blasted pueblo, nobody pays much attention to stray cowpokes," growled Calder. "I can't get over the way that trick was pulled last night. Never heard tell of the like."

"Nor did I," Slade admitted. "It was a novel wrinkle for fair. I recall an incident of a steamer being wrecked on a crib full of rocks built up in a channel, but that was run of the mill compared to last night's incident.

"It was so simple, but so utterly ingenious. It was a foregone conclusion that the pilot would try to beach his ship before it sank, and that the crew, taken utterly unawares, would be in no condition to fight back. Onto the deck, shooting everybody who got in their way, and the devils would have cleaned the safe and hightailed, with nobody knowing where they were headed for."

"And if you hadn't lined us up like you did, it might have been another story," the sheriff said. "I get a cold feeling down the backbone when I think of what would have happened had we gone fooling around that trail with the horned toads holed up the other side of it."

"As I said last night, Estevan really deserves the credit—for tipping us off that something was in the wind," Slade pointed out. "I guessed completely wrong what they had in mind. I'll admit I didn't feel any too good about the business right from the beginning. A widelooping was the obvious thing to expect, and I've learned to distrust the obvious. Well, it all worked out fairly well despite the escape of the one I'm convinced is the real head of the outfit."

"You figure he'll cut loose again soon?" asked Calder.

"Assuredly," Slade answered. "For one thing, an outlaw leader must keep his men well supplied with spending money, and last night he missed a good haul. Also, losing four of their number didn't boost the morale of the others—shook their faith in him, as it were. It's up to him to do something to counteract that. Undoubtedly he is clever and imaginative, and daring, but there are certain basic angles he cannot afford to ignore. Because of these we will be hearing from him soon. Who is he? That's your question; you provide the answer. So far I haven't one."

The sheriff growled and mumbled and fetched coffee from the back room. "Doc will be here in a couple of hours to hold an inquest," he said. "He'll set on that poor devil Dixon Lanham says was one of his hands. I'm expecting Lanham and his bunch any minute."

Estevan and the deputies arrived first. They accepted coffee and sat down to wait. Several more town people scrutinized the bodies of the outlaws, with negative results.

A little later Dixon Lanham and his men put in an appearance.

The Bar L owner's eyes were red-rimmed as from lack of sleep and he appeared listless. Which interested the sheriff. Lanham glanced inquiringly at the bodies. Slade nodded to Calder and the sheriff obliged with a graphic account of the previous night's incidents, to which Lanham listened intently, shaking his head from time to time as the tale progressed. When the sheriff paused, he bent an admiring glance on Slade.

"An excellent piece of work," he said. "A little more of the same and perhaps we'll have peace hereabouts for a change. I sure hope so. I rode patrol last night and had only a couple of hours in bed before setting out for town. I'm shorthanded and can't expect the boys to work all day and then be sashaying around all night, so Phillips, my range boss, and I handled the chore. I left Phillips in bed; no sense in him breaking up his rest to attend the inquest; he wasn't with us when we learned poor Duke had been murdered."

"No reason for him to attend," Slade agreed. "Well, here comes Doc and his coroner's jury, so we'll get this over with."

The inquest was brief, as was to be expected. The posse was commended for doing a good chore on the outlaws. It was ruled that Duke, the slain cowboy, met his death at the hands of parties unknown, and the sheriff was advised to run down the varmints as quickly as possible. Court adjourned.

Lanham and his men decided a few drinks at the Blue Bell were in order. Estevan drifted out like a shadow, the deputies following. Slade and the sheriff relaxed for a bit with more coffee.

"Well, where do we go from here?" asked Calder.

"We don't," Slade replied. "All we can do is sit back and await developments, which I have a hunch will come soon enough."

"I wonder if that hellion was riding patrol last night," the sheriff remarked meditatively, referring to the Bar L owner.

"No reason to doubt his word, so far as I can see," Slade answered.

"Maybe not," Calder grunted, "but he looked to me like he'd been doing some harder riding than just ambling around over the range."

"I fear you see what you desire to see," Slade smiled.

The sheriff snorted, and glanced at the clock. "Well, how about the Blue Bell and a bite to eat?" he suggested. "Court proceedin's always make me hungry."

"Guess one excuse is as good as another," Slade said. "Okay, let's go."

As they neared the saloon, Calder remarked, with a chuckle, "Funny how this rumhole got its name. When he first opened up, Boyer figured to call it the Blue Hell, which would have been a sight more fittin', but he decided some of the town folks might be offended and settled for Blue Bell. Rumhole keepers are always a mite loco."

"A very euphonious name," Slade commented.

"Whatever that means," said the sheriff. "Newfangled cuss word of some kind?"

"We'll let it go at that," Slade answered smilingly. "Anyhow, he puts out good chuck."

"Uh-huh, especially when *El Halcón* is eating here and the kitchen help do their damndest," countered the sheriff as they entered and made their way to their usual table.

"I'll tell the boys so they can dish up something

extra special," said Boyer and hurried to the kitchen.

When the food arrived it was all Boyer claimed for it, and despite his declaration that he was getting round as a porcupine, the sheriff did full justice to his portion.

Lanham and his men were still at the bar, evidently feeling they might as well make the most of the trip to town. He appeared to have perked up considerably and was chatting in an animated fashion with his hands.

Their plates emptied and shoved aside, Slade rolled a cigarette, and the sheriff hauled out his pipe. For a while they sat smoking in silence, full fed and at ease. Suddenly Calder exclaimed, "Look out! Here comes trouble!"

Slade had already noticed the entrance of big, bad-tempered Charge Grundy with his swagger and his truculent eyes. He rose to his feet.

Grundy, with half a dozen of his hard-bitten hands trailing after him, headed for the bar. He had almost reached it when he came face to face with Dixon Lanham. He stiffened, hand dropping to his holster; Lanham's hand was already on his gun butt.

Slade was across the room and between the two men in four giant strides.

"How are you, Charge?" he asked pleasantly.

Grundy stared. Then, his wrath suddenly changed to joy, he let out a bellow, "Slade! So you came back! Feller, am I glad to see you!"

He threw his thick arms around Slade and gave him a bear hug. "Well! Well!" he chortled. "If this ain't plumb fine!"

Lanham and his hands were staring at the tableau. Abruptly, Grundy remembered them and turned to the Bar L owner, his face darkening again. But before he could open his mouth, Slade spoke again, "Charge, I recall you once saying that if you could ever do me a favor, for me not to hesitate in asking it, no matter what it might be."

"You're darn right, and I meant it," said Grundy. "After you saved my life and risked your own to do it, I'd be a prize blankety-blank-blank to refuse you anything."

"Okay," Slade said. "You can do me one right now."

"Name it!" replied Grundy. "What is it?"

"Just this," Slade said, his voice suddenly all music, "Shake hands with Mr. Lanham."

Grundy's jaw dropped. He stared dazedly. Lanham also stared. Then Grundy, the impulsive, bellowed, "By gosh! I'll do it. What do you say, Lanham?"

The Bar L owner met Slade's smiling eyes, and held out his hand. Grundy seized it in his big paw and they shook heartily.

"That's better," Slade said. "Now let's not have any more loco feuding over a business matter that can easily be settled amicably. When honest men start gunning for each other, they lay the field wide open to the owlhoot brand."

"We'll drink on it," said Lanham.

"Service!" bawled Grundy. "Drinks for all of us. You can buy the next round, Dixon. Belly up, Slade."

"I'll take coffee," the Ranger replied, flashing his white smile. He returned to the dazed sheriff.

"Well, guess now I've seen everything," declared Calder. "Wouldn't have believed it possible to get those two horned toads together. Suppose this writes Lanham outa the picture as a suspect?"

"Not altogether," Slade replied soberly. "There are still a few loose ends to tie up where he is concerned, although from the beginning I've been a mite doubtful of him being mixed up in anything off-color. But it still hasn't been explained why somebody tried to murder him over in Matamoros. Well, we'll see. You'll recall I was for a while undecided where Grundy was concerned, the last time I was here."

For a while they sat smoking and talking. At the bar, the Bar L and B Cross C hands were jabbering together and clinking glasses.

Slade viewed the scene with pleasure. "Something gained," he remarked to Calder. "At least we won't have a range war on our hands, which could have easily occurred with that pair with their bristles up and on the prod against each other."

"And that you can say a couple of times," the sheriff replied with fervor. "Enough trouble as it is. Hey! Listen, they're at it again!"

Sure enough, the owners had indeed raised their voices in altercation.

"You take it, Charge," said Lanham. "Be okay with me."

"I won't," Grundy disclaimed in injured tones. "You keep it."

"Gentlemen," Slade called across the room, "suppose you designate that disputed strip as open range and let it go at that."

"That's a notion," said Lanham. "What say, Charge?"

"Sounds good to me, Dixon," replied Grundy. "Oh, he's always right; no getting ahead of him."

They clinked glasses.

The sheriff shook with laughter. "Remind me of two misbehavin' school boys when the teacher speaks," he chuckled. "Well, if you do write Lanham off as a total loss, who have we got to suspect?" he added.

"Nobody," Slade replied. "Not a soul, so far as I can see. We'll just have to keep hunting and hope for a break."

"We got a sorta good one last night," Calder said cheerfully, "but I still can't get over how that scheme was worked. As I said, never heard tell of the like."

"Yes, it was clever," Slade agreed. "And showed an unexpected knowledge of hydraulics. The trap was set in exactly the right place, with the line from the post diagonalled so that the force of the explosion would tend to throw the vessel toward the bank rather than away from it. A few yards farther downstream the channel veers away from the bank, rather sharply. Had the trap been set just a little downstream, the boat would have been carried away from the bank and sunk where they couldn't reach her. A nice bit of engineering on somebody's part."

"Guess you should know," said the sheriff, "seeing that such folks as Jim Dunn, General Manager of the big C. & P. Railroad System, says you're the best engineer that ever rode across Texas."

"A slight exaggeration, I fear," Slade replied smilingly.

However, despite Slade's disclaimer, the sheriff was not too far wrong. Shortly before the death of his father, which occurred after financial reverses had occasioned the loss of the elder Slade's ranch, young Walt had been graduated with high honors from a noted college of engineering. He had expected to take postgraduate courses in certain subjects to round out his education and better fit him for the profession he still hoped to make his life work.

But all that for the time being was impossible. He was forced to alter his plans accordingly, and when Captain Jim McNelty, with whom he had worked some during summer vacations, suggested he come into the Rangers for a while and pursue his studies in his spare time, he was not averse to the notion.

So Walt Slade became a Texas Ranger. And long since he had gotten more from private study than he could have hoped for from the postgrad. Soon he became eminently fitted for the profession of engineering and as time passed, he received numerous offers of lucrative employment from titans of the business and financial worlds whom he encountered in the course of his Ranger activities.

But meanwhile, Ranger work had gotten a strong hold on him, providing as it did so many opportunities to right wrongs, do good, and help the deserving, and he was loath to sever connections with the illustrious body of law enforcement officers. He was young. There would be plenty of time to become an engineer later on, he thought. He'd stick with the Rangers for a while longer.

Which was how the situation stood when Sheriff Calder made his remark that night in Brownsville.

9

Although the Blue Bell was crowded and doing plenty of business, Fats Boyer, the owner, found time to join Slade and the sheriff for a few minutes.

"Mr. Slade, I don't know how you do it," he said. "I was reaching for my shotgun when you stepped between them. Figured we were due for a ruckus and no mistake. I don't know how you do it."

"They were amenable to suggestion," Slade replied.

"Uh-huh, and I've noticed folks are in the habit of accepting *El Halcón*'s suggestions, figuring it's healthier to do so," Boyer returned dryly.

Slade smiled and did not pursue the discussion.

The night was wearing on, and a little later the Bar L and B Cross C outfits trooped out together, shouting good nights to Slade. Confident that everything was under control, for the time being, at least, he and the sheriff relaxed in comfort.

"Yep, looks like we are going to have a peaceful night for a change," Calder remarked. "I hope so."

But he was doomed to disappointment. Both were glancing at the clock and planning their next moves when in the distance sounded a prolonged crackle of gunfire.

"What in blazes!" exclaimed the sheriff. "Sounds like the Battle of Shiloh all over!"

"It's down in the lower town, toward the bridge," Slade said as the guns continued to blast away. "Guess we'd better go have a look."

Things were indeed quite lively in the lower town. A group of seven or eight horsemen had trotted their mounts across the bridge from Matamoros. As soon as they had reached Brownsville, they began racing their horses through the streets, yelling and shooting.

Windows were smashed. Bullets thudded into walls. People dived wildly for cover, and some suffered superficial flesh wounds. Still letting off bullets in every direction, the raiders circled around through almost deserted streets, reached the bridgehead and went pounding across the span, whooping derisively, before the aroused citizens of Brownsville could arm and retaliate. It had all happened in a matter of minutes.

When Slade and Calder reached the scene of tumult, they found an angry crowd assembled at the bridgehead, shouting and cursing.

"Those blankety-blank hellions from Matamoros!" an informant bawled in answer to the sheriff's questions. "Looking for trouble, are they? We'll give 'em trouble!"

"Hold it, I don't intend to have any loco ruckus cut loose here if I can prevent it, and I think I can," Calder warned. "Something mighty funny about all this. Stay right where you are, all of you."

Slade said nothing for the moment, his eyes fixed on the span and the lights of Matamoros.

Now Webley and the other deputy had joined them and the crowd was under control.

Slade turned to the sheriff. "I'm going across to Matamoros," he said. "I want to see Estevan and try and learn what this was all about. As you said, something funny about it."

"I'm going along," said Calder.

"Okay," Slade agreed. "Let's go!"

Calder spoke to the deputies. "Keep an eye on those loco jugheads," he ordered, motioning to the crowd, which had been reduced to mutters.

As they headed up the approach, somebody called, "That's Mr. Slade, the feller they call *El Halcón*, with the sheriff. He'll straighten things out. Take it easy, boys."

The sheriff chuckled.

"Yes, very strange," Slade remarked as they hurried down the south incline. "Appears to be a deliberate attempt to create animosity between the two settlements. But why?"

A crowd had gathered on the south river bank, pointing, exclaiming, staring across the stream. Slade wasted no time with them, but led the way to La Luz, where they found Dolores with a nice case of the jitters, the composed Estevan keeping her company.

"I know not the meaning," he replied to Slade's question, in his usual laconic fashion. "Men ride across the bridge. We hear shooting on the other side of river. Men ride back, and west on the Camino Real. Here they did not shoot, did not speak, just rode."

"Which would indicate," Slade said, "that they were not from down here. Otherwise they would have ridden south. But who?"

"Maybe another blasted *libertador*," growled the sheriff.

"Possibly," Slade conceded, "and from north of the Rio Grande. Estevan, see if you can locate the police chief and bring him here."

Estevan nodded, and drifted out.

"Well, thank goodness you weren't mixed up in this one," Dolores said to Slade. "When he heard the shooting, I was sure you would be."

"Missed out on this one," Slade replied. "Got there just a little late."

"It happens too seldom," the girl said morosely. "Oh, well, you always seem to come out on top."

"Exactly," said the sheriff.

Dolores wrinkled her nose at him and flounced to the dance floor, where she was needed, for people were trooping in from the river bank. The cantina was already crowded and business booming.

Shortly, Estevan reappeared with the *Jefe Politico*. The old Chief of Police nodded to

Slade and the sheriff and sat down, accepting a glass of wine.

"I know not," he said. "Here we were as surprised as north of the river doubtless you were. I cannot understand it. But sure I am that none from Matamoros took part in the atrocity."

"My conclusion," Slade remarked. The chief nodded.

"Were there any serious injuries?" he asked.

"I gather a couple of scratches were the only casualties," Slade replied. "Either very fortunate or they didn't shoot to kill, for some reason or other."

"Do you believe it was the same *ladrónes* who killed the two Texas range riders?" queried the chief.

"It is possible," was Slade's decision. "Part of the campaign to create friction between Brownsville and Matamoros. In fact, I rather think so."

Dolores, who had been conferring with the orchestra, returned to the table. "Walt," she said, "you've got to sing for us. You haven't yet and everybody wants you to."

The chief, who loved good music, heartily endorsed the suggestion. Sheriff Calder added his voice.

"Looks as if I have no choice in the matter if I'm to hope for any peace tonight," Slade acceded. He walked to the little raised platform, where the orchestra leader was waving a guitar. Many of the crowd knew what to expect and talk died down to a hum, ceased altogether as Slade accepted the guitar, made sure it was tuned to his liking, and stepped to the edge of the platform.

For a moment he stood silent, his eyes roving over his expectant audience. Then he flashed the white smile of *El Halcón*, threw back black head and sang, his great golden baritone-bass filling the room with melody. Now softly sweet as rose petals floating on still water. Now deep and powerful as a river thundering in its sunken gorge. The ceiling lifted, the walls fell away, and before the eyes of his entranced listeners stretched the hills and the valleys, the mountains and the plains, the silver coil of the streams, and all that makes Earth fair. And the flaming stars that light the Great White Throne!

Enchantment? Witchery? No! Just the magic of a truly great voice that alchemized simple little songs into gems of marvellous beauty. That brought dreams walking down the path of reality to find snug harbor in men's hearts.

Amid a roar of applause that set the hanging lamps to dancing, Slade returned the guitar to its owner, smiled at the hand-clapping, shouting crowd, and made his way back to his table.

"The singingest man in the whole Southwest," murmured Dolores.

"Doesn't cover enough territory," said the sheriff.

And at a dark window square not in line with where Slade was sitting for an instant a blurred face glared in with eyes that glittered hate! Hate! Hate!

10

The night wore on and the crowd began to thin. Alden Drake, the lawyer and land speculator, sauntered in, nodded to Slade and the sheriff, and made his way to the bar. Slade thought he looked a bit weary. He wore riding clothes that were dusty and had very likely been visiting some of his clients. He had a couple of drinks and departed.

Dolores came over from the floor. “It’s late and I’ve had enough of this place for the time being,” she announced. “I’m going to change and then we’ll cross the bridge together. Okay, dear?”

“We’re walking,” Slade pointed out.

“Then I’m walking, too,” she said and trotted off to the dressing room.

Estevan got up and glided out.

They all crossed the bridge without incident, as Slade had expected, for he knew that again they were “convoyed” by Estevan and his *amigos* with the thirsty knives.

It appeared that things had quieted down in the lower town, for there was nobody around the bridgehead, and they continued through the almost deserted streets and reached Jackson Street, where Calder said good night.

• • •

Early the following afternoon, Slade sat alone in the sheriff's office, conning over the hectic occurrences in the course of his short period in Brownsville. His thoughts were far from satisfactory.

But he felt he had accomplished something. Doing away with the threat of a ripsnorting range war between two salty outfits was not to be lightly disregarded. That situation had been as explosive as the dynamite that blew out the river steamer's bow. The slaying of the four outlaws who attempted to rob the steamer also helped.

But there were several unanswered questions that irritated him. Why had Dixon Lanham's cowhand, Duke, been drygulched? Why had an apparently innocuous range rider been knifed to death on a Matamoros street? As had been two others before him. And why had somebody tried to murder Dixon Lanham? Those incidents just didn't seem to make sense.

As to the raid on the lower town the night before, the simple answer was that somebody was out to create trouble along the Border. But once again, why? Of course, the abortive risings south of the river always provided opportunities for robbing and looting. But conditions now were different from what they had been only a few years before. Such a raid on Brownsville as Cheno Cortinas had staged was impossible. And who would profit from trouble along the river, and how?

Well, back of all the incidents was undoubtedly a motive, and it was up to him to learn the motive. Find the motive, says the book, not a printed book, of the Rangers, and you are well on the way to corralling your man.

"Altogether a nice kettle of fish, to paraphrase an old saying," he remarked to his cigarette tip. "And how to get the fish out before they spoil or boil is at the moment beyond me. Oh, well, maybe I'll get a break, or make one." He took a deep drag and pinched out the butt.

"Get a break, or make one," he repeated. "I've a notion it is up to me to try for a little 'making'!"

He headed for Shadow's stable.

"Going to take a little amble," he told the big black, who appeared pleased at the prospect.

Cinching up, he led the cayuse out and mounted. A little later, found him riding west on the trail. He glanced back several times, although he did not think there was much danger of being followed, then faced to the front and continued on his way, studying the land over which he passed. Finally Santa Rita and La Paloma were behind him and after a bit he was approaching Dixon Lanham's land. He began paying even closer attention to his surroundings.

"For centuries the Rio Grande has been depositing silt all along this area," he told

Shadow. "The land is very fertile in consequence. All it needs is more water. Yes, more water. Well, we learned something from our old *amigo*, Jaggers Dunn, that may tie into the problem we've got to solve. Never can tell, and I'm beginning to wonder a mite."

Slade knew that this had been the route followed by the forty-niners in the course of the gold rush to the far west. Great numbers had landed at Port Isabel and converged on the then straggling village of Brownsville, where they had outfitted for the long journey to California. Thousands had thronged the town, awaiting transportation on the little river steamers that would take them to the head of navigation.

Others, too impatient to wait for the steamers, had outfitted and streamed up the military road laid out by General Taylor's engineers. Still others, sensing greater possibilities nearer at hand than in California, had remained and become pioneer citizens of Brownsville—thus assuring their descendents of prosperity, and in many cases wealth. It was here that Charles Stillman had laid the foundation of what would be one of the greatest fortunes and banking houses of America.

"And from this area will eventually come more 'gold' than was dug from the California hills," Slade told Shadow.

He rode on, until he knew he was passing over

Dixon Lanham's holding. Obeying a sudden impulse, he turned from the trail and rode north by slightly west, remembering approximately where the old M Lazy P ranchhouse, formerly owned by Potter Mays and now Dixon Lanham's Bar L *casa*, was located.

The sun was slanting well down the western sky when he sighted the building, bathed in the mellow glow and appearing to wear the complacency of the aged.

However, it was not so "old" as formerly. Lanham had evidently done quite a bit of repair work and freshening up. There was little doubt but that he was a good cattleman and knew his business. Slade had been favorably impressed by the clumps of Bar L cows he'd passed. A little later, he rode into the ranchhouse yard.

Lanham himself, who was puttering about the yard, glanced up at the sound of hoofs, stared, cut loose a whoop of greeting. "Well, well, this is fine!" he exclaimed as he hurried forward to shake Slade's hand. "Didn't expect you to visit me, but I'm sure glad you did."

"Was riding west on the trail, looking things over, and decided to drop in on you for a few minutes," the Ranger explained.

"Fine!" Lanham repeated. "Light off and come on in the house. I'll have your cayuse taken care of. Blazes, but he's a beauty!"

He let go another whoop. A wrangler came

hurrying in answer, was introduced to Shadow and led the big black to a stall and oats. Slade and Lanham entered the comfortably furnished living room.

"Take a load off your feet," the rancher invited, gesturing Slade to a chair. He whooped still a third time, "Mike!"

A moment later an old Mexican appeared. He stared at Slade, bowed low.

"This is Mike, my cook," Lanham introduced. "Mike, fix us a snack and coffee, will you, please. You've heard me speak of Mr. Slade; this is the man himself."

"I am honored," the old man murmured, with another bow.

"*Gracias*, Miguel," Slade said, and added a few more words in flawless Spanish, which evidently pleased the old fellow greatly. With a third bow, he pattered back to his kitchen.

"Been with me for years," Lanham explained. "Was with me on my holding over on the Sabine. Don't know what I'd do without him. See he recognized *El Halcón*," he added with a chuckle. "He had plenty to say, all of it good, when I told him of meeting up with you."

"Nice of him," Slade said. He glanced around. "See you've been doing quite a bit of fixing up," he commented.

"Yes, I've been busy at it," Lanham admitted. "I like it here and I'm here to stay. Not getting any younger and I've had enough of jumping from one place to another. This is my third holding, and my last. Came pretty near not getting it," he added with a chuckle.

"How's that?" Slade asked.

"When I approached old man Mays, having been told the place was for sale, he told me another feller wanted to buy him out just a few days before. But the feller wanted to make a down payment and the rest on time. Mays wanted to buy a spread over east, close to his folks, and was sorta hesitating, figuring he wouldn't have enough *dinero* to tie onto the place over east that he wanted. I was pretty well heeled right then, having sold my place on the Sabine, and when I offered to put down cash on the barrel head, Mays took me up on it. Guess I was lucky to show up when I did."

"In my opinion you were," Slade said. "It's a good holding and will very likely be worth more later on. Did Mays mention who the fellow was who wished to buy him out?" he asked casually. Lanham shook his head.

"Nope, he didn't. Just said it was a feller who 'peared to know his business. I wasn't interested and didn't ask anything more about the feller. Well, how's things in town?"

Slade told him of the raid from across the bridge.

Lanham whistled. "What a loco-sounding

thing," he said. "Reckon we missed it by just a little. Any notion what it was about?"

"Nobody seemed to know," Slade replied non-committally.

"Maybe some sort of a private feud, like Grundy and I were trying to have," Lanham hazarded. "Folks do loco things when they get mad."

"That is true," Slade agreed and did not commit himself further. Actually, he was beginning to get a hazy notion about a number of things that had appeared unexplainable.

A moment later, Miguel called them to the snack, which proved bountiful and tasty, and to it they both did full justice.

"You inspire him," chuckled Lanham. "This is prime. The boys will be in for their surrounding soon," he added, glancing out the window at the scarlet and gold of the sunset. "And I'm going to ride patrol again tonight. Feel I'm duty bound to keep an eye on things, considering what all has happened hereabouts of late. Quite a few cow critters missing from the various spreads, including some from mine."

"Mind if I ride with you?" Slade asked.

"Would be plumb pleased to have you," Lanham replied heartily. "I've a notion you'd see things I'd miss."

Everything taken into account, Slade thought it quite likely. When the plates were empty, he called thanks to the cook, who was rattling pots and pans in preparation for the hands' evening meal, and he and Lanham retired to the living room with coffee and cigarettes.

"You brought your own hands with you when you took over, I presume," the Ranger remarked.

"That's right," answered Lanham. "Mays took the few he had over east with him. I could use two or three good riders, but so far, I've not been able to tie onto any to my liking. Reckon some are liable to drift along any day, though."

Slade thought it likely, but resolved to give anybody Lanham managed to hire a careful once-over.

Shortly, the hands rolled in. Josh Phillips, the range boss, whom Slade had not met, was introduced, and after a bit of casual conversation, Slade and Lanham cinched up and rode out through the deepening dusk.

As they rode, Slade carefully studied his surroundings and arrived at several definite conclusions. Among others, that a large portion of the south range was lower than the normal surface of the river.

However, the approaches to the stream were high and firm and there was no danger of an overflow, nor had there been for many, many years. Which he found interesting.

They rode steadily, in no particular direction, although they gradually worked northward, passing waterholes and little streams where cattle congregated, drinking and feeding on the lush grass.

It was a still night without a breath of air moving, but not unpleasantly warm. The sky was slightly overcast but enough starlight filtered through the cloud wrack to render large obstacles clearly visible for some distance. At least to the eyes of *El Halcón.*

"I like to ride at night, always did," Lanham observed.

"I can understand that," Slade replied, "but I'm going to give you a little advice. Don't be riding around at night by yourself. Always have somebody with you. Same applies to the daytime. Better to have a couple of the hands along if practicable."

"Why—why do you think something might happen to me?" Lanham asked in surprise. "I sure can't see who would do anything now that Grundy and I have gotten together."

"Frankly, I don't know definitely," Slade conceded. "But some queer things have been happening hereabouts of late, and I think you would be wise to do as I say."

"If you say so," Lanham agreed. "That why you decided to go along with me tonight?"

"To an extent," the Ranger admitted. "I also wanted to look things over and get a better notion of the spread."

The hours passed and it was getting along toward midnight when they reached a point from which they could see the shimmer of a broad gray band stretching down from the north.

"Trail from Edinburg and Pharr," Lanham remarked, jerking his thumb toward it. Slade nodded; he was familiar with that trail.

They rode slowly toward the trail. Where they approached it, the track suddenly dived into a rather shallow but long dry wash, the greatest depth of which was perhaps ten feet below the surrounding prairie. Doubtless when the trail was first beaten out, the wash was much shallower. But the going through the depression was easy except right after a hard rain, and the trail did not bypass the work but held to its original course. The lips of the wash were fringed with a straggle of rather high chaparral growth.

At the edge of the wash they turned their horses and rode north, paralleling the trail. They had covered some little distance when Slade abruptly reined in and sat gazing northward.

"See something?" Lanham asked.

"Yes," the Ranger replied without turning his head. "A bunch of cows coming down from the north, fast."

Lanham peered with puckered lids. "I can't see anything," he said.

"You will in a minute," Slade predicted, his gaze still fixed on the north.

"By gosh! You're right," Lanham exclaimed. "What kinds of eyes have you got, anyway?" he marvelled. "Cows, all right, and headed this way, fast. What is this, a widelooping?"

"Looks sort of that way," *El Halcón* answered, still not turning.

"Say!" Lanham said, "those must be some of my critters. Blast it! they're not going to get away with it!"

He started to ride forward, but Slade's hand on his bridle detained him.

"Hold it!" the Ranger snapped. "There are six or seven men shoving those beefs along. You'd be riding into a hornet's nest and get blown from under your hat. Hold it, and let me think a minute."

Fuming and swearing, the rancher obeyed, glaring at the oncoming herd, which was still quite a distance away, but dimly visible to even his eyes.

"All right," Slade abruptly said, "back down to where the trail drops into that dry wash. I believe, with a little luck, we may be able to turn the table on those enterprising gents. I'm sure they haven't spotted us; showing no signs of alarm. Okay, ride fast."

With the horses speeding, they quickly reached the wash. Slade continued for about half its length, then pulled to a halt and said, "Okay, unfork and lead the cayuses forward a little ways, where they should be safe from flying lead. Right! This should do it. They're out of sight from down below. Now back up the wash a little and hole up in the brush where we have a good view of the floor of the wash. It's narrow and the riders will bunch back of the herd. Let the herd get nearly past before we make a move. I'm a law enforcement officer and have to give the devils a chance to surrender. They won't take it, so shoot as fast as you can and yell as loud as you can. Even if you don't hit anything, shoot fast, and yell loud. Understand?"

"I do," Lanham growled. "And I figure to shoot *straight,* too."

11

Now they could hear the bawls of the irritated cattle. A little later, the thudding of their hoofs.

"Better than a hundred head, I'd say," Slade estimated. "Would have been a nice haul had they gotten away with it."

"And if it wasn't for you, they would have," Lanham said. "Think we can handle them all right?" he added nervously. "Odds against us are a mite lopsided."

"Barring an unlucky accident, I don't see any reason why we shouldn't," *El Halcón* returned composedly. "The advantage appears to be all on our side. They are mounted, we are on foot. We will be holed up in the brush, they'll be in the open. And don't overlook the element of surprise—that counts for plenty. Shift each time you squeeze trigger, and hunker down. At that angle they are almost sure to shoot high. Quiet now, they're getting close."

Tense and ready, they crouched in the brush. Lanham was sweating profusely despite the coolness of the night, but grimly determined. Slade was his normal cool and calculating self.

"Get set!" he breathed. "Cows coming into the wash."

Another moment and the dark shapes of the

cattle began streaming past. Slade waited an instant. Then, as seven horsemen bulged into view, his voice thundered through the night, "Up! You're covered! In the name of the State of Texas!"

Below sounded astounded exclamations. Slade saw hands streaking to holsters. He drew and shot, left and right. Lanham's gun boomed beside him.

"Let 'em have it, boys!" Slade roared. "Don't let one of the sidewinders get away!"

Lanham echoed with a nerve-shattering screech as he fired as fast as he could squeeze trigger, and continued to yell his loudest.

Two saddles were emptied by that first bellowing volley. The hush of the night was split to smithereens by the eruption of horrendous sound. The crash of the guns, curses, yells, the cries of the stricken, the bawling of the terrified cattle, and the screams of frightened horses blended in an uproar to shudder the stars.

Dodging, ducking, shifting, Slade shot with both hands at the dimly seen forms below. Answering slugs whined past, showering him with twigs and leaves. Slugs fanned his face, but he was untouched. He fired again and a third widelooper went down. His guns and Lanham's boomed together, and there was a fourth empty saddle.

There were still three of the raiders erect, but

they had had plenty and more than plenty. They whirled their mounts and streaked back up the wash. Both of Slade's hammers clicked on empty shells. He slammed them into their holsters and sped to where he had left Shadow, whipping his Winchester from the boot.

But by the time he was back away from the growth enough to line sights, the fleeing trio were but vanishing shadows. He sent several slugs in their general direction but with little hope of scoring a hit. Tucking the rifle under his arm and reloading his Colts, he rejoined Lanham who, now that all was over, looked a bit white and shaken, even in the starlight, which had brightened considerably.

His eyes on the motionless forms at the bottom of the wash the while, Slade rolled and lighted a cigarette which he handed to the rancher.

Lanham accepted it with a wan smile. "Guess I'm just not used to a thing like this," he said, puffing hard on the brain tablet.

"You came through like a veteran," Slade complimented him.

"Uh-huh, maybe so," Lanham replied. "At first I was so mad about my cows being rustled right under my nose that I forgot to be scared. But while we were waiting for them to reach the wash, all of a sudden, I realized that two men going up against seven desperate hellions wasn't exactly poker. Oh, I was in a couple of lead-trading ruckuses when I was younger, but that was man to man, and not tackling odds of better than three to one."

Slade smiled, and changed the subject. "I slipped," he remarked. "Should have laid my long gun beside me instead of leaving it in the boot. Gave the other three a chance to escape. Well, guess none of those horned toads down below are playing possum. Suppose we look them over."

Browsing about in the growth, Slade secured a bit of dry and resinous wood that made a fairly satisfactory torch. By its light, they scrambled down the side of the wash, which wasn't very steep, and they began to examine the four dead men.

Average brush-riding Border outlaws, giving the appearance of being somewhat more intelligent than most, was Slade's verdict. But Lanham exclaimed over one with a cunning fox face. "I remember this hellion," he said. "He came up to me in the Blue Bell and braced me for a chore of riding. I didn't like his looks and told him I wasn't hiring right then. What in the devil!"

"Would have been a plant, eased into your employ to get the low-down on conditions, and quite likely to keep tabs on your movements," Slade said.

"But why should anybody do that?" Lanham asked in bewildered tones.

"Men, as a rule, are creatures of habit," Slade

explained. “When riding, for instance, they usually follow certain routes. Which, if known, would make a drygulcher’s work easier.”

Lanham’s expression became more startled than bewildered. “You mean you think somebody is out to kill me?” he asked.

“I’m fairly positive of it,” Slade replied. “That’s why I warned you not to go riding around alone.”

“But who?” the rancher wondered.

“To that question, I’d very much like to have the answer which, unfortunately, I haven’t got,” the Ranger answered. “Well, I see your cow critters have quieted down and are grazing, so we won’t bother about them. The horses these wind spiders rode are standing up at the head of the wash. We’ll strip the rigs off them and turn them loose. You can pick them up later, good looking beasts. The bodies and everything else we will leave as is; I want the sheriff to see them this way. He’ll be at your place early tomorrow and you can guide him here. Now let’s head for your *casa*, and you go to bed. I’m ambling to Brownsville.”

“It’s a long and lonely ride,” Lanham protested. “Why not wait till morning.”

“It isn’t so very late, and Shadow will make light of it,” Slade replied. “Let’s go.”

Slade paused at the Bar L *casa* long enough to drink a cup of coffee. Then he continued on his way under a starry sky that was now wonderfully clear. And before he reached the trail, a late moon soared up in the east and flooded the rangeland with silvery light, making the scene almost as bright as day.

At the trail, Slade drew rein and again sat for several minutes studying the area.

A little way to the west was a rather shallow, almost circular depression. It was nearly a quarter of a mile in diameter and had doubtless at one time, years before, been a small lake or pond. Slade regarded it with the eye of an engineer.

"Shadow," he said, "things are beginning to tie up. I still don't know on whom to drop my loop, but I'm pretty sure I've got the motive, which is plenty important. Okay, jughead, sift sand. Be late before we reach town, and everybody will be wondering what in blazes has become of us."

The big black, sensing oats in the offing, set off briskly, gradually increasing his pace. Slade let him have free rein.

With Shadow in a hurry to get to his stable, the trip to town was made in good time, and it still lacked several hours till dawn when they reached Brownsville.

When he entered the Blue Bell, after caring for his horse, Slade found, as he'd expected, Sheriff Calder, with Dolores and Estevan keeping him company, awaiting him.

"All right, let's have it," demanded the sheriff.

Slade obliged with a brief recital of the night's events.

The sheriff said things, under his mustache, in deference to the presence of a lady. Estevan showed regret that he hadn't been along. And Dolores shuddered, and shook her curly head resignedly.

"All in all, just a lucky break, spotting the rustlers where we did, with the advantage ours," Slade concluded.

"A darn lucky break for Lanham," grunted the sheriff. "Suppose he'd been riding around out there alone and had run into that bunch?"

"If he had, he wouldn't have anything more to worry about in this world," Slade replied. "As it was, he didn't lose any cows and enjoyed a pleasant evening."

"You and your notions of pleasure!" said Dolores.

"After I knock off a little ear pounding, I'll round up Webley and Gus and fetch the carcasses in," announced the sheriff. "Will have Lanham ride back to town with us, for chances are Doc will want to hold an inquest later in the day."

"And have Phillips, his range boss, or one of his hands accompany him," Slade said.

"Okay," Calder replied. "And now I vote we call it a night."

To which suggestion nobody disagreed.

12

There was no lack of excitement in Brownsville when the sheriff arrived with his grisly cargo. Quickly the office was jammed with eager listeners who wanted to hear Lanham's vivid account of the night's happenings. Slade finally managed to escape out the back door to avoid the plaudits with which he was showered.

The inquest, however, was rather a repeat performance which he could not completely bypass.

After the expected verdict was rendered, the crowd dispersed and the bodies were removed for burial. The sheriff closed and locked the door, and he and Slade went into executive session, as it were.

"Well, one thing is sure for certain," Calder said, "you're thinning them out. Today's batch makes eight all told, according to my counting."

"Yes," Slade agreed, "but I figure there are more of them, and plenty more available in this section. And with the head of the outfit, whoever he is, running loose and active, we can expect more trouble, and soon."

"Don't you figure the two setbacks he got will tone him down a bit?"

"Not likely," was the Ranger's opinion. "Specifically for two reasons. He needs money to further an ambition I feel sure he is nurturing. And, I believe, it is logical to assume his pride is touched, and something his sort can't abide. For quite a while, I gather, everything has been coming his way, one successful raid after another. Being brought up short like he was in the last two attempts won't sit at all well with him, and he'll be out to even the score.

"No, I don't think a couple of setbacks will curb his activities. Just the opposite, I'd say. We'll be hearing from him soon, on that you can safely wager," Slade said positively.

"And you still have no notion who the hellion is?"

"I'm afraid not," Slade replied ruefully. "He is certainly doing a beautiful chore of covering up."

"Think he was with the wideloopers last night?" Calder asked.

"That is my opinion, with little on which to base it," *El Halcón* answered. "It seemed to me that a couple of the three who escaped were tall, but even as to that I couldn't say for sure. Right at that moment the cloud wrack had thickened and the light was very poor. Well, guess I'll have to put Estevan on the trail; that young rapscallion has an uncanny ability to ferret out what is apparently concealed, what *is* concealed from most everybody else."

"Yes," agreed the sheriff. "I don't know how he does it."

"One reason is that he concentrates on a certain objective to the exclusion of all else," Slade explained. "What has happened before and what will happen in the future concerns him not at all. Whereas we, as a rule, have a number of things in mind. Because of which we are liable to overlook the obvious."

"Sounds sorta complicated, but I reckon I get what you mean," said Calder. "Estevan plays his cards as they fall and don't bother his head about the next deal."

"I guess that's one way to put it," Slade smiled. "How about some coffee."

"Coming up," said Calder, and suited the action to the word.

They drank the coffee in silence, Slade gazing thoughtfully out the window, the sheriff regarding Slade.

Yes, Estevan was good at ferreting things out, but Calder was willing to bet that *El Halcón* would come up with a solution to the problem before the knife man.

Finally pushing his empty cup aside, Slade stood up. "Not long until sunset," he said. "I'm going to take a walk."

"Okay," replied the sheriff. "We'll have dinner together at the Blue Bell, right?"

Slade nodded agreement and strolled out. For some time he wandered about town, studying faces, listening to talk, gradually working his way toward the bridgehead at the foot of Fourteenth Street.

He entered the Last Chance and contacted Sturm and Teresa.

"Yes, some folks are still a bit het up over what happened the other night," Sturm said. "But you and the sheriff cooled 'em down considerable. Now most people figure it was just a bunch of ordinary hellions raising the devil on their own, and that the folks of Matamoros had nothing to do with it. Of course, I've been spreading word of that around, and so has Teresa."

"Nice of you and it helps," Slade told him. "And I really don't believe there'll be a repeat, now that the other night turned out to be a fizzle."

"Expect you're right," said Sturm. "You usually are."

Promising to drop in again soon, Slade left the Last Chance and sauntered up town. Suddenly he slowed his steps. He was approaching an office, across the plate glass window of which was legended, *Alden Drake, Counsellor at Law.*

And standing in the doorway was Alden Drake himself. He waved a cordial greeting.

"Come in and have a drink with me, Mr. Slade," he invited. "Understand you've been a busy man of late. Keep up the good work, we can stand more of it. Come on in."

Slade accepted the invitation. Drake waved

him to a chair and repaired to the back room for a bottle and glasses and water. Slade glanced at the rows of books on the shelves.

The majority dealt with the law and kindred subjects, but there were some of a different category. Among them, Slade noted Watson's *Elements of Applied Geology*, Gibson's *Hydraulics and Its Application*, and Wedstoe's *Principle of Irrigation Practice.* He dropped his gaze as Drake reentered the room.

Drake proved to be a good conversationalist, and Slade listened with interest to his discourses on various subjects. Also, with amusement, for he quickly realized that Mr. Drake was on a little fishing expedition.

Finally, a baffled look shadowed the lawyer's face for a moment. He was learning what others had learned before him, that Walt Slade would talk pleasantly and freely, but that he wouldn't tell you anything. When Slade stood up to go, he knew just as much about *El Halcón* as when the Ranger had sat down. *And no more!*

"Thank you for the drink," Slade said. "It's been a pleasant interlude, but I'll have to leave you. I'm meeting Sheriff Calder at the Blue Bell for dinner."

"May drop in there later myself," Drake replied, adding casually, "Expect to cross the river to La Luz tonight?"

"Quite likely," Slade conceded.

"Good!" said Drake. "May see you there, too; I like the place."

"It is always gay and colorful," Slade agreed. His eyes were very thoughtful as he walked through the deepening dusk to the Blue Bell.

Boyer's place was also quite gay when Slade entered. And he quickly learned that the frustrating of the wideloopers the night before was the chief topic of conversation. He sighed resignedly as he made his way to the table, where the sheriff awaited him.

However, Boyer managed to steer away most of the inquisitive so that the two peace officers could enjoy their meal without too much interruption.

Lanham, who had attended the inquest, was at the bar with Phillips, his range boss, talking with acquaintances. He joined them for a moment. "Decided to spend the night in town and not take that lonely ride through the dark," he explained.

"A wise decision," the Ranger said.

"Think it'll be all right if we ride across to La Luz a little later?" the rancher asked. "A gal over there I sorta like."

"If you wait and ride with the sheriff and myself," Slade replied.

"Okay, we'll do that," Lanham promised.

The sheriff speculated his back as he returned to the bar. "Think there's really a chance somebody may try to do him in?"

"Well, you'll recall it was tried once," Slade reminded. "The hellions might figure to have better luck next time."

Calder regarded him curiously for a moment, hesitated, bolted a morsel of meat, and said, "You're looking mighty smug. Finally figured out who's the he-wolf of the pack?"

"I at least have a hazy notion," Slade conceded.

"Then it's but a matter of time until we drop a loop on the sidewinder," Calder said with confidence.

"But it's liable to be like trying to drop a loop on a greased pig," Slade replied. "He's a slippery customer. But he made one of the unexpected and tiny slips the outlaw brand seems always prone to make. Wouldn't have meant anything had I not already gotten a fairly good notion as to the motive. That suddenly tied the loose ends together. We'll discuss it later."

Calder grunted and applied himself to his food. "Hello!" he exclaimed a moment later. "Here come Grundy and his bunch."

The B Cross C owner glanced about, spotted them, gave a whoop and came plowing to the table. "Heard something about it," he said. "Rode in to get the low-down."

"Over to the bar and talk with Lanham," the sheriff directed. "He'll tell you exactly what happened. No use asking this young hellion. Accordin' to him, he just had all the luck and got the breaks. The sidewinders fell off their cayuses and cracked their skulls on the rocks. You know him!"

"*Do* I know him!" chortled Grundy. "Okay, me for Lanham."

He headed for the bar and was quickly listening to Lanham's account of the adventure, shaking his head and chuckling, and shooting admiring glances at *El Halcón.*

"So Lanham is plumb out of the picture, eh?" remarked the sheriff.

"Definitely," Slade replied. "In fact he was never really in it except in a vague sort of way; wasn't the right type. There were just some seemingly mysterious and unexplainable complications connected with him that were perfectly clear once I'd stumbled onto the motive. Lanham is a rather salty gent, but comparing him to the real head of the outfit is like comparing a pet tomcat to a hooched-up mountain lion.

"Strange, but when a really able and intelligent man goes wrong, he is the very worst type to deal with. Without conscience, without fear. Utterly callous and ruthless. And all too often afflicted with the blood lust, getting real pleasure from brutal murder. That's the kind of critter we are up against. He's playing for big stakes and doesn't intend to let anything stand in his way, if he can prevent it," Slade summed up.

"Oh, well, you've gone up against that sort

before and always came through with bells on," said Calder. "I ain't worried. Old Jim McNelty was right when he said you don't only out-shoot the devils, you out-think 'em, too. Guess brains is what counts most in the long run. Let us drink!"

Which they proceeded to do—Slade coffee, the sheriff a generous helpin' of redeye.

Lanham, who had evidently finished his recital of the widelooping episode, for Grundy's benefit, began glancing suggestively at Slade.

"Seems anxious to get moving," *El Halcón* remarked to Calder. "Figures to have business across the river."

"He's got woman on the brain and is old enough to know better," snorted the sheriff. "Oh, well, there's no fool like an old fool, as I've been telling myself for quite some time now. Well, guess we might as well humor him. Feel like moving around a mite myself."

"Okay, by me," Slade said and stood up, beckoning Lanham, who responded with alacrity. Phillips also came along.

"May see you over there a little later," Grundy shouted.

Slade was watchful as they rode across the bridge, although he thought there was little danger of an attack on four armed and vigilant men; that would be just a little too crude. If an attempt was made against them, one or all, it would be something subtle.

They threaded their way through the busy streets to La Luz and entered, leaving their horses at the rack. Lanham immediately drifted to the edge of the dance floor. Slade, Calder, and Phillips sat down at a table, with Amado hurrying to serve them and Dolores trailing along.

A few minutes later, Slade noted that Lanham was on the floor, dancing with a very pretty little thing with flaming red hair and contrasting black eyes.

"That's Juanita," Dolores said. "She's nice, and all right in every way, but nobody, man or woman, had better try to put something over on her. She hasn't got that crackling red hair for nothing."

"Another Irish-Spanish combination, I'd say," Slade remarked. "Dynamite done up in small packages."

Dolores giggled, and didn't contradict.

While Lanham and Juanita were dancing, three men, tough looking customers, entered. Their eyes swept the room, focused on the dance floor. Slade saw their heads draw together in low-voiced conversation. They hesitated an instant, then made their way to a table near the floor, sat down, and ordered. Again heads drew together, eyes glinted toward the floor. Slade watched them.

Lanham and Juanita danced three numbers, then repaired to a table, sat down and ordered. Wine for the girl. Whiskey for Lanham. Now, Slade saw, the eyes of the three men were regarding the couple.

Calder and Phillips were deep in talk. Slade eased out of his chair and unobtrusively glided forward a few paces, pausing at the edge of the dance floor, from where he had a clear view of both tables.

Abruptly one of the men stood up, strode to the table occupied by Lanham and Juanita, his hand on his gun butt. Slade heard his truculent growl to Lanham, "You! Get the hell away from that girl, and stay away!"

Lanham's head flung up, his eyes glowing with anger, and he started to rise. But he was at a distinct disadvantage, at the other's mercy, in fact.

But the fellow hadn't counted on Juanita. Her little hand flicked out, closed on the brimming whiskey glass. The next instant, he got the contents of that glass squarely in his face. He howled, pawing madly at his eyes as the fiery liquor scorched them. His two companions leaped to their feet, cursing, hands darting to their holsters. One got his gun out. The room quivered to the crash of a shot.

The gun wielder yelled with pain and doubled up, gripping his blood spurting hand between his knees. His iron clattered across the floor. His companion stood rigid.

And with good cause. He was looking into two unwavering black muzzles, one wisping smoke, and back of those muzzles, the eyes of *El Halcón*!

Before Slade could speak, Amado, with a bellow of wrath, dashed forward. He and his floor man seized the unsavory trio, rushed them to the swinging doors, and out. To where, Slade saw, Estevan and his *amigos* were waiting.

Followed scream after scream of agony, and the beat of staggering feet moving away from the cantina. Slade didn't go out to see what was happening. He didn't want to see.

A minute later, Estevan sauntered in, wiping his blade with a bit of cloth. He shook his head. "We did not slay those *ladrones*, *Capitán*," he said. "But hereafter, each will be known as *La Cicatriz*—The Scarred One!"

"*Gracias*," Slade replied, and drew a deep breath. Estevan and his followers were the most loyal of friends, and utterly dependable, but they were also just a little terrible.

13

The room was in an uproar for fair, everybody shouting at once, nobody seeming able to figure what the ruckus was about. Calder and Phillips were flanking Slade on either side, ready for business. Dolores ran to Juanita, who, not at all perturbed, was patting Lanham's hand and chattering angrily in two languages.

Slade strolled over to join them. "See?" he remarked pointedly to Lanham who, for the second time in less than twenty-four hours, looked a bit shaken.

"Yes, I see," the rancher replied slowly. "Thanks once again."

"Thank *her,*" Slade said. He reached down and rumpled the red-haired girl's bright curls.

She smiled up at him, shyly. "The touch of *El Halcón* is a benediction!" she murmured softly.

But gradually order was restored. Lanham was supplied with another drink. Slade, Phillips, and the sheriff returned to their table.

"A very nice try," the Ranger remarked. "A row over a girl, Lanham reached first, and the other shot in self defense. Would have gotten by with it, especially with the help of a really smart lawyer."

"Wouldn't think there was such a thing over here," Calder growled. Slade smiled, and didn't argue the point.

"Guess the sidewinders didn't figure on you," the sheriff said.

"I doubt if they knew we were here, their attention being focused on Lanham," Slade replied.

"Reckon that's the answer," agreed Calder. "Otherwise they wouldn't have tried it. By the way, that was quite a distance to shoot a gun out of a hellion's hand. Don't you ever miss?"

"Sometimes, *inside* the other's gun hand," Slade replied smilingly.

The sheriff "got" it, and chuckled.

"Say! That little redhead is something!" enthused Phillips, the taciturn Bar L range boss, who seldom spoke unless spoken to.

"Yep, she's all of that," replied Calder. "Another gal to ride the river with." He glanced at Dolores.

"*Gracias*, I accept the compliment for both of us," she smiled.

"And maybe Lanham ain't as big a fool as I figured him to be," the sheriff added thoughtfully. "Guess he could do a lot worse. And from the looks of 'em right now, I've a notion they'll end up pulling in double harness."

"Juanita is lucky," said Dolores. "*He* won't go riding off to the ends of the earth."

"But look at the fun it is when he comes riding back." Calder pointed out.

"If and when," Dolores countered. "Well, back to the floor. Now business is really booming. Takes a nice row to fill the place. Uncle Amado should pay you a salary just to come in, Walt."

"All rumhole owners get rich," snorted the sheriff. "I don't know what the world's coming to."

"But look at all the fun sheriffs have," said Dolores and skipped away before he could frame a suitable reply.

Slade enjoyed the exchange of thrusts, but his mind was occupied with something more serious than persiflage. Looked like he had another problem on his hands, the problem of keeping Dixon Lanham alive. Incidentally, he figured he needed to learn a little more about the Bar L owner and resolved to question Lanham relative to certain details. He believed he already had the answers, but it would be well to obtain confirmation.

Charge Grundy and his hands roared in, which did not tend to quiet things down. Immediately they got the story of what happened, from Lanham, and showered both Slade and Juanita with praise, which the Ranger felt he could well do without.

"Anyhow, though," he said to the sheriff, "we won't have to worry about crossing the bridge;

we'll have the nucleus of an army accompanying us."

"If the hellions don't blow it up under us," grumbled Calder. "Wouldn't put it past them." Slade thought there was small danger of that, the span being impervious to anything short of a carload of explosive.

The night wore on. The crowd began to thin out, for there was a day of work ahead. The orchestra packed its instruments. The roulette wheels spun for the last time. The card tables dealt a last hand. Lanham and Juanita whispered together a few minutes before she joined the other girls in the dressing room. Dolores appeared in her riding costume, glancing suggestively at the clock. A few minutes later, Slade and the others left La Luz, secured their mounts and headed across the bridge.

They were descending the north incline when the sheriff suddenly leaned forward in his saddle, staring. At the foot of the span stood a group of at least a dozen men, scattered out. The starlight glinted on the rifles some held.

"Looks like maybe we're due to have some trouble," Calder said grimly. "Okay, keep the gal in the middle. If it's trouble they're looking for, they'll get it."

Slade, who had been scrutinizing the group, spoke. "Don't think there'll be any trouble," he said. They rode on, slowly, the sheriff, Grundy, and the others with hands close to their holsters.

Slade, with Dolores beside him, still held the reins, and with his other hand rubbed his jaw.

Suddenly the sheriff gave vent to an outraged roar, "What the blankety-blank blue blazes are you loco hellions up to? What's the meanin' of this?"

Slade chuckled.

"We figured it was those devils pullin' another raid," a voice called back, apologetically. "We just got ready for 'em."

"Well, it ain't," the sheriff bawled. "And what the blankety-blank do you mean by takin' the law in your own hands! You leave that for the authorities. Now scatter away from here 'fore I fill the calaboose so full of you, you'll hafta spit up in the air. Get goin'!"

The armed crowd began dispersing, knowing that Calder was as good as his word, and more so.

"Heck!" shouted Charge Grundy, in an injured voice, "I thought it was a reception committee waitin' to welcome us back to town."

That created a laugh and eased the tension. Even the sheriff grinned crustily.

"Something of an anticlimax, but it indicates an attitude that must be changed," Slade remarked as they rode on to seek their rest.

Calder was still grumbling over the incident of the night before when Slade joined him at the office the next day.

"The whole business don't seem to make sense," he complained. "Why should somebody want to kick up trouble between the two towns?"

"The answer is comparatively simple," Slade replied. "If folks here start blaming people the other side of the river for everything off-color that takes place, who will profit? The outlaws, of course. It's similar to starting a ruckus between two outfits, with each sure the other is back of the depredations suffered, and thus giving the owlhoots a clear field in which to operate—as I pointed out to Lanham and Grundy. Understand?"

"Guess I do," Calder conceded. He regarded Slade for an instant, then shot a question, "Well, who is he?"

Slade smiled, knowing exactly what the sheriff meant, and dropped his bombshell.

"Alden Drake!"

The sheriff was seated comfortably in his tilted-back chair, his feet on the desk. His boots hit the floor with a thud and he jerked forward, staring.

"Wha—what the blue blazes!" he sputtered. "Walt, you don't mean it!"

"I do," Slade replied. "Alden Drake is the head of the outlaw bunch operating in the section."

"But—but what makes you think so, how do you know?" demanded the bewildered peace officer.

"Drake made a mistake, one of the little slips

his kind always seem to make. He invited me into his office for a drink."

"Will you please tell me what the devil you're talking about?" snorted the thoroughly exasperated sheriff. "Caught onto him 'cause he invited you into his office to have a drink!"

"Exactly," Slade smiled. "Okay, here goes. But I'll have to preface my explanation with a brief dissertation on the geological and hydraulic peculiarities of the area. Doubtless due to some terrestrial disturbance of the past ages, the south section of Dixon Lanham's holding, the Bar L, is lower than the land to the east and west. In the nature of a shallow and wide trough, as it were. Many years ago, the Rio Grande, in times of high water, overflowed onto that lowland. Overflowed and constantly deposited silt. As a result, the land, under a rind of grass, is amazingly fertile. All it needs to grow really magnificent crops is water."

"All that hell needs to make it okay, I guess," interpolated the sheriff.

"A rather far-fetched parallel, but could apply," Slade conceded.

"In addition," he continued, "just north of the river there was in those days a small lake. But the river cut its channel deeper and built up its banks over the course of many, many years. As a result, there was no longer an overflow, and the little lake dried up. However, it left a depression which will provide a storage basin or reservoir for water impounded against seasons of drought. Which is important; constructing impounding basins is a costly business. A great advantage to have one ready to hand. Beginning to understand, now?"

"No, I don't," growled Calder. "Where does Drake come in?"

"Very shortly," Slade answered. "Now I'm going to tell you something that I want you to keep strictly under your hat."

He paused to roll and light a cigarette, his hearer waiting expectantly.

"Very shortly," he resumed, "an extensive irrigation project will begin in this area, under the supervision of the Alexander Company, a most reputable concern, that built the irrigation system at Laredo. Their engineers will quickly realize the advantage of the condition I just described and will pay Lanham a whopping big price for that south section of his holding. Lanham will be able to make out if he never sells another head of stock. All right, here comes Drake, in just a little while.

"Until I had familiarized myself with the terrain and understood the significance of the prevailing conditions, I was at a loss as to why somebody was so anxious to kill Lanham. Then I learned that just before Lanham acquired the spread, somebody else, whether Drake or his emissary I don't know which, tried to buy it.

“However, the would-be purchaser didn’t have enough money to meet the asking price but proposed a down payment and the rest on time. That didn’t exactly suit Potter Mays and he put the fellow off while he considered the proposition. Then along came Lanham, who was able to lay down the full amount Mays asked, and Mays sold to him.

“Incidentally, just to bolster my opinion, before he rode home today, I asked Lanham did he have relatives who would inherit his property did he happen to pass on. He told me his only living relative was a sister over east, married to a bank manager who would not be interested in a cow factory and would be glad to sell his wife’s inheritance to the first bidder, which would be Drake. Now do you begin to understand?”

“I understand why somebody wants to do in Lanham, but I don’t understand how it all ties up with Drake and him asking you in to have a drink,” the sheriff replied.

“You will in a minute,” Slade predicted. “Fine! I had the motive, but I hadn’t the slightest notion on whom I was to drop my loop. I’d been beating my brains out endeavoring to single out somebody with the geological and hydraulic knowledge necessary to be able to appreciate the significance of the conditions I have described, with no success. I hadn’t given Drake a thought, although there were certain little incidents relative to him and his behavior I should have noted.

"While waiting for him to procure drinks, I saw on a shelf, among his law books, several volumes dealing with geology, hydraulics, and irrigation. Highly technical works that could be understood only by a person thoroughly versed in such matters. Right then I knew Alden Drake was my man.

"And in addition, other items to which, as I said, I had given no thought occurred to me. How he was present both times just before an attempt was made to kill Lanham, his undoubted interest in my unworthy self whom he considers a menace to his plans and who must be gotten rid of as quickly as possible. And so forth. Now do you see it?"

"Guess I do," sighed the sheriff. "The usual way you work, making plenty out of what nobody else would give a thought to. Yep, you sure make out a case against the blasted sidewinder."

"But without one iota of proof that Drake is mixed up in anything off-colored. Nothing but theory on my part, and playing a hunch," Slade said.

"You'll get it," Calder declared. "Just thought of something. Why was poor Duke, Lanham's cowhand, drygulched?"

"Duke," Slade explained, "was the unfortunate victim of mistaken identity."

"Yes?" prompted the sheriff.

"Yes," Slade replied. "The drygulcher was after Lanham. Duke happened to be much the same height and build as Lanham. As I mentioned at the time, the bullet that killed him was fired from quite a distance. When Duke happened along, the drygulcher, not being close enough to get a really good look at him, mistook him for Lanham."

"I see," said Calder. "And, by gosh! Now I understand what you said last night about the horned toad who aimed to kill Lanham—that he would have pleaded self-defense and would have gotten away with it with the help of a really smart lawyer."

"Exactly," Slade said. "Of course Drake couldn't practice south of the river, but he could advise the local attorney representing the killer just how to handle the case. With Lanham dead, the fellow would have given himself up to the local authorities, with his two companions swearing that Lanham had pulled first. And the possible prosecution, did it come to that, would not have been strong, the Matamoros authorities taking but a mild interest in ruckuses between cowmen from the north of the Rio Grande. Oh, he's plenty shrewd and hardly ever misses a bet. Shrewd and farsighted and undoubtedly has connections somewhere. Was able to learn about the contemplated irrigation project here, which is supposed to be a good deal of a secret. Well, we'll see. Perhaps he'll make another slip and give us a break. So far, the breaks have been largely in his favor. Twice, I'd say, he came close to getting his comeuppance. In the course of the attempt to rob the river steamer, and during the try at widelooping Lanham's cows. But both times he managed to slip out of the loop."

"Figure that by any chance he knows you are a Ranger?" Calder asked.

"Highly doubtful, in my opinion," Slade replied. "Much more likely he subscribes to the *El Halcón* yarn and possibly figures I'm here trying to horn in on what he's started. Hope so."

"You would!" snorted the sheriff, adding hopefully, "maybe Estevan and his knife men marking those three hellions like they did last night may throw a scare into him, showing him there are gents just as salty as he sets up to be."

"I fear that, unfortunately, he is not the sort to scare so easily," Slade differed. "We'll be hearing from him soon, you can count on that. It is logical to presume that he needs to amass more money, if he hopes to acquire the Bar L ranch when he manages to do away with Lanham. Also, his followers' morale can stand a little boost. They may be getting a mite jittery after what has happened of late."

"They'll be more than jittery 'fore we get through with them," growled the sheriff. "But it puts Lanham on a rather hot spot," he added.

"Yes," Slade agreed, "but he's very much on

the alert now and is taking no chances. He'll always have a couple of his hands with him when he's riding. Because of that I don't think he needs fear anything as crude as a shot from the brush. Where we've got to keep an eye on him is here in town, and especially when he goes to see the little redhead across the river. I'll have a couple of Estevan's boys ride herd on him, which should help."

"You're darn right," agreed Calder. "They sure don't let any grass grow under their feet. I'd just as soon have the devil after me as them."

"Hardly an overstatement," Slade agreed.

14

The sheriff fetched steaming coffee from the back room and for a while they sat smoking in silence. Then Calder abruptly remarked, "As I've said before, I can't understand how the devil you do it. From practically nothing, you build an airtight case against a hellion."

"And I can't understand how I came to overlook the obvious while beating my brains out and wearing my feet sore trying to hit on somebody who would qualify as leader of the bunch," Slade rejoiced. "You will recall that after the attempts to rob the steamer and to rustle Lanham's cows, Drake appeared giving indications of a hard night. And I gave it no thought. And tieing onto him was just a pure fluke of luck."

"That and being able to understand what you saw," said Calder. "I wouldn't have given those blasted books a thought."

"Because you never had the training that would enable you to realize their significance when joined with other factors," Slade explained. "Incidentally, I learned something from Charge Grundy this afternoon that also helps. After a little probing, Charge told me it was Drake who dropped a hint concerning that slice of land he and Lanham were arguing about. He mentioned that the survey made when Potter Mays took over the holding, years ago, was done with a hundred-foot rawhide rope, two riders switching ends of the rope, and that it was done on a rainy day. Wet rawhide stretches and each switch of the rope took in quite a bit more distance than it should have, which caused an overlap onto the acreage that became Grundy's B Cross C holding.

"Charge, being hot-tempered and impulsive, braced Lanham about it and they had a row. I gather Drake adroitly refrained from making any accusations of wrongdoing; just mentioned to Grundy that he heard it to be the case, which was enough to set Charge off."

"With Drake hoping Grundy and Lanham would get into a corpse and cartridge session and Lanham be killed by Grundy, who has a mighty fast gun hand," guessed the sheriff.

"Exactly," Slade said. "Might well have worked out that way."

"Chances are it would have if you hadn't sorta clipped the spurs of those two fightin' cocks," Calder replied.

"Possibly," Slade conceded. "Grundy *is* mighty fast on the pull."

"Uh-huh," said the sheriff, "I recall he tried to shade you, the first time you met, and got a hole through the top of his shoulder for trying it. I can still hear folks sayin', 'Good gosh! Shaded Charge Grundy! Charge didn't even clear leather!' Yep, Grundy had quite a reputation as a fast gunhand."

Slade smiled and changed the subject. "So we have our suspect. All we need to do is corral the gentleman, which is liable to prove a somewhat hefty chore; he's a slippery customer."

"Think he may figure you suspect him?" asked the sheriff.

"I doubt it," Slade replied. "I don't see any reason why he should. So keep your face straight when you contact him. The longer we manage to keep him deceived on that score, the better. Interesting, he is the second off-color lawyer I've contacted. Another of the same calibre represented the notorious Land Committee at Laredo; was the head of the bunch, in fact.

"Well, not without precedent," Slade continued. "So was John Wesley Hardin a lawyer and a school teacher who, had he stayed straight, might well have ended up a professor at a great university. Never can tell where the lightning will strike."

He was silent a moment, then said, "I'll line up Estevan to keep tabs on all Drake's moves; may get results."

Calder grunted agreement, and poured more coffee. "If we could just hit on what the horned toad will be up to next," he remarked.

"That would help a lot," Slade replied. "And very likely prevent another killing. I'd say that right now Drake is in a mood to show mercy to nobody, and a nice sadistic murder would soothe his injured feelings. Well, after I finish my coffee, I'm going to take a walk. Be dark before long. And then I'll stop at the Blue Bell. Lanham and Phillips decided to stay in town another night. Not much to do at the spread, and Lanham figures he can stand a bit of rest. I'll sort of keep an eye on him myself until I line up Estevan and his boys."

"Okay," said Calder. "I'll see you at the Blue Bell later."

Slade spent quite a while strolling about aimlessly. He could always think better in the open air, and he figured he had plenty to think about.

All very well to be confident in his own mind that Alden Drake was the moving spirit behind the depredations that had been committed in the section, but that wouldn't be enough to convince twelve gentlemen in a jury box; something more definite was needed. How to acquire it? At the moment Slade had not the slightest notion. That Drake and his devils would strike somewhere soon he was sure. But unless he was able to anticipate the move and guard against it there wasn't much to be gained from his conviction.

He passed Drake's office. It was unlighted and the door was shut, with Drake nowhere in sight. Maybe the hellion was already operating.

A thought that did not serve to tranquilize *El Halcón*'s mind.

After a short visit with Burley Sturm and Teresa, in the Last Chance, he headed for the Blue Bell through the deepening dusk.

When he entered, the sheriff had not yet arrived. Nor was Lanham in evidence.

"Was here just a little while ago," Fats Boyer replied to Slade's question as to the rancher's whereabouts. "Said his range boss and him were going to ride across to Matamoros."

For a moment, Slade stood digesting this bit of disquieting information. Then, he said, "When the sheriff drops in, please tell him I'll be seeing him before long," he said to Boyer and headed for Shadow's stable. He experienced an uneasy premonition that everything was not as it should be with Lanham running loose in Matamoros. Besides, he wished to request Estevan and his boys to keep a watch over the Bar L owner.

He cinched up with speed and crossed the bridge at a fast pace. Arriving at La Luz, he paused at the rack, dropped the split reins to the ground and entered the cantina. Glancing around, he spotted Phillips, the range boss, at the bar alone.

"Where's Lanham?" he asked abruptly.

"Why, Mr. Slade, you must have almost passed him in the door," Phillips replied. "A feller came in with word from the little redheaded gal that she wanted him to come to her place for a few minutes and walk her back to the cantina. Said her little house was right around the corner on Calle 12. The one with the big tree in front. Say! Isn't that her coming out of the back room now? Don't see Lanham."

It was. The girls usually entered by the back door on the way to their dressing room.

Slade was through the swinging doors before Phillips could speak further.

"And the loco coot fell for it!" he muttered as he headed for Calle 12 at almost a run. He was familiar with the street, as he was with most of Matamoros, and believed he knew the approximate location of the house in question, his attention once having been drawn by the stately tree that indeed grew in front of it.

He *was* running when he whisked around the corner. There were a few people on the street, who stared at him in astonishment as he sped past them.

Another moment and, by the glow of a street light, he spotted Lanham just turning into the yard. He increased his already flying pace. He dared not shout to the rancher to warn him, for Lanham would very likely call back and precipitate the action Slade was convinced was in the making.

He reached the yard, swerved into it. Lanham was knocking on the door. Slade distinctly heard a muffled voice call to him to come in. As the rancher turned the knob, Slade bounded forward, seized him by the shoulder and hurled him back and to the ground.

"Stay there!" he snapped as he himself went backward several paces in the same ripple of movement, weaving and ducking the while.

Feet pounded the floor inside the house. The door was flung open and two men bulged out, guns in hand, cursing and exclaiming at the sight of him.

Slade drew and shot as both outlaw irons spat flame. A slug ripped through the crown of his hat. Two more shredded his shirt sleeve, just graining the flesh. He fired again and again, and still again, not for an instant ceasing his weird slithering dance.

Then he lowered his smoking Colts and peered through the powder fog at the two motionless forms sprawled on the ground. He whirled to Lanham who, half-stunned by the force of his fall, was trying to regain his feet.

"Slade!" he gasped as the Ranger seized him by the arm and hauled him erect. "What in—"

"Come on, away from here!" *El Halcón* interrupted, propelling him, lurching and staggering, to the street.

A patter of steps and Estevan loomed before them, swinging his blade by the point, two of his *amigos* trailing behind him.

"*Capitán*!" he panted. "Saw you we, the cantina leaving, but for feet wings you grew. You overtake we could not. All is well?"

"Everything under control," Slade replied as they shouldered past a couple of staring men who dodged away from that swinging knife. "Please send one of your boys to find the *Jefe Politico* and bring him to La Luz. And Estevan, from now on, please ride herd on this loco hombre whenever he is in town."

"Assuredly, *Capitán*," said Estevan, who had recovered his breath. "Both be done shall." He spoke to one of his followers, who hurried on ahead.

The still badly shaken and thoroughly bewildered Lanham found his voice. "Slade," he asked, "was—was that another attempt to kill me?"

"It certainly was, and close to being successful," the Ranger replied grimly. "A very neat trap, delectably baited with—a woman."

"Good heavens!" Lanham exclaimed in consternation, "Where's Juanita?"

"Safe in La Luz; don't worry about her," Slade reassured him. "I saw her come in just before I left."

"And she didn't send for me?"

"Of course not," Slade replied as they turned the corner. "It was an excellent bit of timing. The messenger got to you while she was heading for the cantina by the back way. The other two slipped into the house right after she left it. Easy enough to get in, even with the door locked, by gents with the know-how. Well," he added, "you'll have a lot less to worry about from now on, with Estevan and his boys keeping watch over you."

Silently, Lanham held out his hand, first to Estevan and then to his follower, both of whom looked embarrassed.

"Inside and to a table as if nothing happened," Slade directed as they neared the cantina. "No talk until the police chief arrives."

They had almost reached the door when Dolores and Juanita came hurrying out. The little redhead gave a glad cry and flung herself into Lanham's arms.

Dolores, instantly sensing Slade's wishes, restrained her. "Quiet, *cara mia*," she whispered. "We will hear what happened, later."

"I understood that something was wrong when Mr. Phillips told us how you rushed out when he mentioned that Juanita had sent for Mr. Lanham, and Juanita said she didn't send for him," Dolores murmured to Slade as they entered the cantina. "We were coming to see if we could learn what. I'm hiding my gun in a fold of my skirt," she added with a giggle. "Makes the hem slip up a little more than it should, but I thought I might need it."

"I've a notion it would please the customers,

if you packed it that way all the time," Slade chuckled, glancing down.

"And that will be enough from you," Dolores retorted.

Taking her cue from Dolores, Juanita was laughing and chattering gaily, Lanham doing his best to follow suit. They sat together at a table and put in their orders, Phillips, the range boss, joining them, but keeping quiet at a word from Lanham.

Speaking in a low tone, Slade gave a terse account of what had happened. Dolores breathed deeply. Juanita favored him with a grateful look. "Much do I owe you," she murmured. "*El Halcón*! the just, the good, the fearless! May *El Dios* ever guard you!"

Walt Slade bowed his head.

15

It was quite a while before the police chief arrived. The girls were on the floor; Estevan had drifted out. Slade sensed from the twinkle he'd seen in his eyes that he would pause at the house on Calle 12.

"Did *Capitán* hear the shooting?" he asked, when he'd returned. He sat down and accepted a glass of wine. "It seems two *ladrónes* into a dwelling broke and must have quarrelled over the loot they expected to get, and fought. Both died. The door we locked, after making sure nothing was taken. The bodies we removed. Both were *Americanos*, *Ai*! It is a wicked world."

Slade did not contradict this astonishing version of the affair, knowing that, as once before, the chief wished to guard him from involvements that might necessitate revealing his Ranger connections. But in answer to his expectant glance, he repeated the story of what really had happened.

The chief nodded approval, and accepted more wine. "Señor Lanham, fortunate to such an *amigo* have," he remarked.

"And don't I know it!" Lanham replied. "If I had as many lives as a cat, I'd owe them all to him."

The chief chuckled at the retort, and offered a suggestion, "Would *Capitán* like to view the bodies? And you also, *Señores*?"

Slade thought the notion a good one, and so did his companions. So, waving goodbye to the girls, who regarded their departure dubiously, they left the cantina and made their way to the undertaker's establishment, which was not far off.

Present there was another gray-haired, distinguished gentleman who shook hands vigorously with Slade. It was the *alcalde*, mayor of Matamoros, another of the Ranger's old *amigos*. He gestured to the stark forms laid out on slabs. "Alas that men should quarrel and fight!" he remarked dolorously, but with a twinkle in his shrewd old eyes.

The dead men were rather unsavory appearing specimens, their faces blotched with vice. Slade did not recall having seen them before, nor did Lanham or Phillips. Which mattered little; he knew his man, and with whom these fellows had associated in life was no longer of more than scant interest.

"*Dinero* from their pockets we took," said the mayor. "To bury them it will pay. On the table, *Capitán*, is all else that was removed."

Slade examined the heap of trinkets such as range riders carry and discovered nothing of significance.

There were a few of the curious loitering in the parlor. Slade scanned their faces in search of the two men they had passed on the way to La Luz, and who had been not far off when the gun battle in front of Juanita's house took place, and failed to find them. Which was not surprising. Citizens of Matamoros were not given to meddling in such affairs, which were considered none of their concern and might involve them in difficulties.

Drawing the *alcalde* aside, he repeated the story of the incident. The mayor, like the chief, nodded approval. "*Capitán*'s hand is sure, for which *El Dios* be praised," he murmured.

Satisfied that there was nothing more to be learned, Slade and his companions said good night to the mayor and the chief and returned to La Luz.

Estevan was now lounging at the near end of the bar, his usual position. Slade paused beside him. "Got another little chore for you, *amigo*," he said.

"Of a certainty, *Capitán*," the knife man replied cheerfully. "Who is to die?"

"I don't think you'll have to go that far, for the present, at least," Slade smiled. "You know the Señor Alden Drake?"

"*Si*."

"Try and keep tabs on him. If he rides off somewhere, try to ascertain in which direction, and let me know at once."

"*Si*," was the laconic response.

Slade joined Lanham and Phillips at their table. "I'm riding to Brownsville," he announced. "Calder will be wondering what in blazes became of me. I'll be back later. Sure you can remain here if you wish," he replied to a question from Lanham. "With Estevan's *amigos* riding herd on you, as I said before, you have nothing to worry about. Yes, I'll have another cup of coffee with you before I go; Dolores is leaving the floor."

Dolores joined them and Slade told her what he had in mind.

"And please try and not kill anybody before you get back," she requested. "It's getting to be monotonous."

"Okay, I'll try not to," he promised carelessly.

When Slade reached the Blue Bell, he found the sheriff really wondering what had become of him or what he'd got mixed up in.

"Was just about ready to ride across and find out," he said. "What did hold you?"

Slade told him.

The sheriff swore with wholehearted fervor. "Women!" he concluded. "The loco hellion's got woman on the brain and ain't good for anything else."

"He was fortunate to have a woman on his left at the table the other night," Slade pointed out. "Otherwise that devil might have done for him before I could get into action."

"Not likely," Calder differed. "Oh, the gal's all right. It's the man you can't depend on. Don't stop to think, just bulges ahead."

"Drake been in?" Slade asked.

"Not so far," the sheriff replied. "One reason I kept hanging around, figuring he might come in. About all I've been doing of late, it seems, hanging around rumholes."

"The advantage of rumholes, as you call them, is that sooner or later most everybody shows up in them," Slade pointed out. "Saves a lot of running around looking for people."

"Guess that's right," Calder agreed. "Anyhow it makes a pretty good excuse. Now what?"

"I'm riding back across the river," Slade replied. "I wish to keep in touch with Estevan, who is on Drake's trail. Hope he has located him."

"All right for me to go along?" the sheriff asked.

"Don't see any reason why you shouldn't," Slade said, knowing he liked Matamoros and La Luz.

Calder secured his horse and they crossed the bridge without misadventure to find the cantina busy and lively but peaceful enough.

The peace endured and Amado closed early.

Lanham bade Juanita a reluctant good night. "Just got to get to the spread and do some work," he told her. "But I'll be back soon."

Dolores giggled as they rode to Brownsville under the stars. "I scent orange blossoms," she whispered to Slade. "Yes, they're both smitten. Guess they could do worse, though," she added with a little sigh.

Late the following afternoon, Estevan strolled into the sheriff's office with what Slade felt was disquieting news. "The Señor Drake is not," he announced laconically.

"No?"

"No," Estevan repeated. "Neither last night nor today has he been seen. His office is closed. In Brownsville nor Matamoros is he, that *Capitán* can rest assured."

"*Gracias*," Slade said. "Keep watching."

"That we will do," Estevan promised, and Slade knew he would be good as his word.

After a cup of coffee, spiked from the sheriff's bottle, Estevan departed.

"Where in blazes can that devil be?" wondered Calder.

"We'll learn," Slade predicted grimly.

However, they did not learn anything during the remainder of that afternoon, nor in the course of the evening that followed.

"And I'd sleep a lot better if we had learned something about the horned toad," Calder growled.

Slade felt somewhat the same way.

16

Port Isabel was about thirty miles by trail from Brownsville. In 1870, a narrow-gauge railroad was built from Brownsville to Port Isabel and was still in service and doing plenty of business.

Port Isabel was primarily a fishing town, and not much of a town at that, featuring corrugated-iron fish sheds. Boats plied between the mainland and the nearby shores of Padre Island, the southern end of which was visible from the beach. Three miles of shallow water separated the island and the port. Among other things, Port Isabel boasted a ramshackle hotel, which also was doing plenty of business.

For already Port Isabel, with its fine fishing, was feeling the influx of tourists that later would invade the area like a swarm of devouring locusts. But unlike the predatory grasshoppers, they would pay well for everything they ate and drank.

So the hotel proprietor thought nothing of it when three men in "store clothes," wearing neatly trimmed beards and carrying what appeared to be cased fishing rods, registered for rooms.

Had the proprietor been a more observant man, he might have noticed that the three wore riding boots. But he didn't, and, the chances are, if he had, he would have paid the fact no mind.

"You just about got in under the wire, gentlemen," he cheerfully told the three. "We're mighty close to being full up, and have been all week. Business is mighty good. Folks dropping in from all over, and I figure it to get even better. There you are, and I'll show you to your rooms."

One of the men, tall, broad-shouldered, with glittering dark eyes, thanked him courteously in a pleasant and cultured voice.

"A real gent, that big one," the proprietor observed to the night desk clerk, who had just come on duty. "Sure talks nice. Well, you won't have much to do tonight except turn away any folks that show up; only one room left vacant."

He glanced at the ponderous iron safe of ancient vintage that stood in a corner of the little office, and rubbed his hands together complacently.

"Plenty of *dinero* in that old box," he chuckled. "Tomorrow we ship it to Brownsville and the bank by way of the railroad. Safer that way than by steamer, which might sink."

Still chuckling at his own humor, he said good night and left the clerk in charge.

It was well past midnight and Port Isabel was sound asleep when the night clerk, dozing at his desk in the semi-gloom of the office, which was lighted by but a single shaded lamp, heard light steps descending the stairs. He started up to see the three bearded men who had registered for rooms the previous evening approaching the desk, carrying their cased fishing rods. One of them had a peculiarly bulging and large canvas sack.

"Checking out, gentlemen?" he asked, stifling a yawn.

"Yes, we wish to get an early start," replied the tall and broad-shouldered individual with the cultured voice.

The clerk nodded, and bent over the register, which was the last thing he would see for quite a while. A gun barrel crashed down on his skull. Blood spurted onto the register and he fell senseless to the floor.

The three men went to work with smooth efficiency. The tall man took a hand drill from the canvas sack, squatted in front of the safe. One of his companions moved toward the stairs, the other to the outside door. Each had a gun in his hand.

The keen steel bit of the drill cut into the soft iron of the old safe almost as if it were cheese. Hole after overlapping hole was drilled around the combination knob, the tiny whine of the drill barely audible.

In a surprisingly short time, the knob was lifted out, the safe door was swung open, and its money contents transferred to the canvas sack.

"Plenty!" the tall man said in a low voice.

"More even than I expected. Okay, that does it. Let's go!"

Without a glance at the unconscious clerk lying with his head in a pool of his own blood, the robbers glided from the office, glanced cautiously around, and hurried to a stand of thicket that flanked the trail leading into the little hamlet.

The tall man whistled a low note. A moment and a mounted man appeared from the growth, leading three saddled and bridled horses. The villainous trio mounted and all four rode west by slightly south at a fast clip.

Dawn had already flushed the sky and the upper rim of the sun was due to appear any moment when an early rising guest came down the stairs, approached the desk, halted in horror at what he saw, and filled the building with his yells.

Followed pandemonium on a grand scale. Aroused patrons, some scantily clad, jammed the lobby-office, exclaiming, swearing, bawling questions nobody could answer. Present too was the proprietor, who slept in the hotel, out-cursing everybody else.

Most fortunately, among the guests was a doctor. He at once went to work on the pistol-whipped clerk.

"Badly hurt," was his verdict, "but I think I can pull him through. All right, some of you, lift him, carefully, and place him on a bed so I can work on him."

Under the doctor's ministrations, the clerk finally recovered consciousness, but could add little to what was already apparent to the eye. He was even vague as to what time the outrage had occurred, and able only to say that it must have been some time after midnight.

Very belatedly, the proprietor thought to send a wire to the sheriff, notifying him of what had occurred.

"Reckon there ain't anything much Calder can do," the proprietor said to the telegraph operator. "The devils got a head start, and nobody knows in what direction they went. About all I can remember about them is that one was big and tall and they all three wore whiskers. Which sure ain't much to go on.

"Yes, blankety-blank them! They made a big haul. A whole week's take and more, and you know the kind of business I've been doing. And some of the boat owners had money in that safe, too. They got puhlenty!"

Sheriff Calder had "puhlenty" to say when he received the belated telegram, none of which would look well in print.

"Well, anyhow we have learned where *amigo* Drake was yesterday," Slade remarked as he and the sheriff conferred.

"You feel sure it was Drake and his bunch?" Calder asked. "Wire don't tell much. Just says one tall, two short, all three wore whiskers."

"Of course," Slade replied. "Drake and two of his followers, wearing false beards, the simplest and most effective of disguises with many old men and young men growing beards. It's an aftermath of the great war. And the hair processors, whose business has boomed since the war, have become very expert in their art. Their products can be told from the real thing by only the most careful scrutiny; the difference would never be noted by the casual observer with no reason to be suspicious. The kind of thing to be expected from the Drake brand. As I've said, time and again, the west is getting a new type of criminal, smooth, farsighted, employing big city methods. Drake is an excellent example. The old-timers would use a sledge hammer or dynamite to open a safe, and in so doing would arouse the whole community. Not the present day operator. His method disturbs nobody and provides him with the opportunity to get a head start after completing the chore. Just as undoubtedly happened in this case. The wire doesn't say so, but I'm ready to wager the robbery occurred hours before it was discovered."

"Well, we'll know about that a little later," said the sheriff. "Wire said the hotel owner will be here on the early afternoon train, which is due in less than an hour; wants to have a talk with me. Maybe able to fill in a few details for us. Wonder how they made their getaway?"

"Very likely an accomplice was waiting in some thicket with horses," Slade said. "That would be the way he worked it. And of course nobody knows in which direction they hightailed. Just about a perfect crime. Which is not supposed to happen. Experience says there is always a clue, some simple angle overlooked. Could be this time. Well, we'll see."

"At least the wire didn't mention anybody being killed," Calder observed. "May learn different, though, when that jigger gets here with his story."

"My surprise is that nobody was," Slade said. "Silence was absolutely necessary to the consummation of the project."

"Expect you're right," the sheriff conceded. "You usually are. I'll fetch some coffee while we're waiting for that coot to show up."

Slade nodded and rolled a cigarette.

"Well, the sidewinder put one over, all right," Calder remarked as he brought in the coffee. "Hit where neither of us paid any mind to."

"That's his big advantage," Slade said. "He knew what he was going to do, while we could only guess. I'll admit I never gave Port Isabel a thought. No bank there, no stage station. Nothing, it would seem, that would provide him with the opportunity to make a good haul. The hotel never occurred to me, although perhaps it should have."

"Wonder if it was just luck he hit the place on a

night when the safe was stuffed with *dinero*?"

"More likely he knew," Slade answered. "As a lawyer and a reputable businessman he was able to learn things. Expect he's been keeping tabs on the place and had the low-down on all the angles. Yes, he put one over; outsmarted us nicely, as he's been doing right along."

"He didn't outsmart you a couple of times, to say nothing of you saving Dixon Lanham's hide from getting an air hole in it," the sheriff pointed out.

"Rather, I got the breaks a couple of times," Slade disagreed. "Both in the case of the attempted steamer robbery and the try at widelooping Lanham's cows."

"Uh-huh, but you sure outsmarted him both times when the showdown came, and that's what counts for my money," said Calder.

With which *El Halcón* could hardly differ.

A little later, the hotel keeper arrived and filled in the details, which tallied very neatly with Slade's deductions.

"No, the clerk wasn't too bad hurt," he replied to Slade's question. "Doctor said there's a slight fracture, but doesn't consider it serious. Guess he was lucky, at that. A plumb wonder the devils didn't stick a knife in his back. Wonder why they didn't instead of just walloping him?"

"A knifed man will sometimes scream," Slade explained. "Whereas a hard blow on the skull will usually elicit only a grunt. And they couldn't afford noise and did just the right thing, from their viewpoint. Never missed a bet."

"Guess that's right," the other admitted, accepting a cup of coffee.

"Figured how much they got?" asked the sheriff. He whistled when the amount was named.

"Hit me rather hard, but I'll make out," the owner said. "Business is mighty good."

"And it will get better and better," Slade predicted. "In fact, I believe an apartment house for the accommodation of the tourists that will be flocking in would be a good investment."

"By gosh! I've a notion you've got something there," the hotel man exclaimed.

And the building he later erected is still standing, and still in use.

"Well," said the keeper, when he had finished his coffee, "I reckon there's nothing more I can tell you, Sheriff. So I think I'll amble over to Boyer's Blue Bell, down a couple of snorts, and then catch the train back to Port Isabel. Good hunting!" He departed, whistling cheerily.

The sheriff hauled out his pipe and lighted it. After it was going to his satisfaction, he remarked, "Now the sidewinder has made a really good haul, maybe he'll lay off for a while."

"Wishful thinking, I fear," Slade answered. "I sincerely doubt it. I believe he still needs more money to accomplish what he has in mind and he won't stop until he gets it."

"Or is stopped," Calder said sententiously.

"Precisely," Slade concurred. "And it's up to us to do the stopping. Anyhow, I feel better now that Estevan and his bunch are on the trail. Drake will not be able to leave Brownsville without them at least knowing which way he's headed. Which could help considerably."

"You're darn right," agreed the sheriff.

"I can't help but feel," Slade said thoughtfully, "that Drake is running short of followers. Perhaps all he has left are the three that helped him rob the hotel, the pair that registered with him and the one who held the getaway horses. Of course, I could be wrong in that."

"How about the three whose faces Estevan and his boys sliced up with their knives?" the sheriff suggested.

"I would say," Slade replied, "that those three, that is if they're still alive, are now quite some distance from this section of Texas, possibly they are gone from Texas altogether."

"Yes? How come?" wondered the sheriff.

"Because," Slade explained, "they are marked men in more ways than one, and suddenly have become liabilities instead of assets. Drake would realize that at once, and they would know he'd realized it. And where gentlemen of Drake's calibre are concerned, 'liabilities' have a nice little habit of quietly disappearing. So, if they got the chance, it is logical to assume they, without delay, would do some voluntary disappearing," Slade summed up.

"The snake-blooded hyderphobia skunk!" Calder exploded.

"Yes, he's all of that, with apologies to the snake and the skunk," Slade said. "Of course, I could be totally wrong in my analysis of the situation relative to those three, but somehow I don't think I am."

For some moments, he sat gazing out the window at the sun-golden street. The sheriff watched him in silence, apparently understanding that something was building in his mind, which he might not want to mention at the moment.

And as a matter of fact, he did have a notion, and with it a certain uneasiness. Slade did not consider himself infallible; he could make mistakes as well as another, and now was not the time for a mistake, when a life might well hang in the balance. Abruptly he stood up. "Going to mosey around a bit," he announced. "May take a little ride."

The sheriff regarded him suspiciously but offered no objection. "Okay," he said, "I've got some paper work to do. Watch your step."

Slade promised and departed. However, he did not wander about the streets, but headed straight for Shadow's stable where he cinched up.

“A little leg stretching is in order,” he told the big black as he headed west on the Laredo trail. “I recall saying that I didn’t think Drake would try anything against Lanham as crude as a drygulching from the brush, but circumstances were a bit different then, and Señor Drake has demonstrated a flair for the unexpected. It is imperative, from his point of view, that Dixon Lanham be eliminated, and soon, if what he has in mind is to be consummated. He hasn’t had much luck in town and may well resort to other methods, crude though they may be.

“So we’ll just play a hunch and make preparation against such an eventuality.”

Shadow snorted agreement and ambled on at a good pace, Slade letting him choose his own gait, for time didn’t mean much as long as he reached his objective before full dark.

17

Across Ezekiel Comb's holding and Charge Grundy's B Cross C, the trail followed the open prairie, which was not adapted to drygulching, and Slade paid his surroundings little mind. But as he neared the point where Duke Ambrose was drygulched, he grew more alert, sweeping the terrain with eyes that missed nothing.

At the post where he'd found Duke's body, he drew rein and studied the slopes.

The one to the south was quite steep, the brush that fringed its crest somewhat ragged. But the one to the north was gentle, the brush beginning a bit above the trail and on the crest, bristling thick against the blue of the sky.

"If something is going to be tried, it will take place right here," he told Shadow. "Not a long-range shot such as did for poor Duke, however. Not by starlight. But from the crest of the north rise, a rider down here would provide an excellent target for a good marksman. Yes, right here it will be the spot. So we'll do a little exploring and see what we can find."

Turning Shadow's head, he rode back east and then, after reaching the eastern terminus of the ridge, skirted it, rode west until he felt he must be opposite the spot where the drygulching of the Bar L cowhand had taken place. He then approached the rise from the north, shooting glances in every direction.

Reaching the north base of the ridge, he dismounted, edged Shadow into the chaparral, and dropped the split reins to the ground. "Okay, stay put," he told the horse.

With this he climbed the slope, not a difficult chore, to the crest, wormed his way through the thick growth to the final fringe, and gazed down at the trail.

His estimate of distance proved to be correct. Almost directly below was where he'd discovered the body of Duke Ambrose, a spot that was within easy rifle range on a clear night.

"Made to order for a holed-up killer," he remarked to Shadow, after descending the north slope. "Of course I may be following a loco hunch, with Drake having no such thing in mind, but somehow I don't think so. Well, now it's up to Estevan and his bunch to keep me lined with the devil's moves. Little doubt but that they will. Let's go, horse."

He rode back to town, in a very thoughtful mood through the deepening dusk.

The night passed quietly. Estevan had nothing to report. "Still he is not," said the knife man. Slade was not particularly surprised; Alden Drake had been a busy man the night before.

The sheriff went to bed early. Slade crossed the river and accompanied Dolores back to Brownsville.

The following day, around dusk, Dixon Lanham and Phillips, his range boss, rode in.

"Figured to go across for a word or two with my gal," the rancher told Slade. "Feel safe here with your *amigos* riding herd on me."

"I think you are—here," Slade replied with a significance that was lost on the Bar L owner.

"We won't be in Matamoros later than midnight," Lanham added. "Plenty of work to do tomorrow."

After he and Calder had dinner at the Blue Bell, Slade made a suggestion. "Suppose you amble over to Matamoros and keep an eye on things there for a while," he said to the sheriff. "I'll stay here, where Estevan will meet me if he learns something he thinks I should know."

"Not a bad notion, I reckon," Calder agreed. "See you later."

Slade did wish the sheriff to keep an eye on things across the river, but he was swayed also by a second motive. If what he had a feeling might happen looked probable, he preferred to handle the matter by himself. He was reluctant to expose the old peace officer to needless danger, and he also believed he could do the chore better alone. Calder was capable and fearless, but what he had in mind required a certain talent for woodcraft that the sheriff lacked, but in which *El Halcón* was a master.

Calder finished his snort and departed. Slade sat on in the Blue Bell, smoking and sipping coffee, watching the swinging doors expectantly.

It lacked more than an hour before midnight when Estevan glided in, sat down, and accepted a glass of wine. "He is," he remarked.

"Yes?" Slade prompted, although he knew very well what the cryptic remark meant.

"*Capitán* will doubtless recall the cantina by the river, which in gathered those five *ladrónes* the night the looting of the river steamer attempted was," Estevan said.

Slade nodded.

"In that cantina," continued Estevan, "the Señor Drake talked with a man. Low they spoke, and what was said I hear could not, but the man the head nodded and nodded, as does one who instructions receive."

Estevan paused to sip his wine, then resumed, "For some time they talked. Then the Señor Drake a little louder spoke, saying that to La Luz he would go. He left the cantina. Hesitated I, but decide did it was best to watch the man, whose looks liked I not. I caught the eye of one of my *amigos*, who stood nearby and he the Señor Drake followed. The man his drink finished in the way leisurely, then he too left the cantina. I followed. At the rack a *caballo* he mounted.

My *caballo* was nearby, ready. So mounted I and followed, at the distance *Capitán* would say discreet. The man crossed the bridge and rode to the trail Laredo, and turned west. And, *Capitán*," the knife man concluded sententiously, "across his saddle bow a rifle he carried."

For a moment Slade sat silent, digesting what he had learned. Then he said, "*Gracias*, Estevan. You did fine. Now go back to Matamoros and keep watch on Drake, watch his every move. Yes, you have helped a lot."

"It is the honor great," Estevan murmured, bowing his head. He emptied his glass and glided out.

For several minutes, Slade sat conning over the details of the plan he hoped to put into execution, there being no great hurry. Lanham would not be likely to cross the bridge for an hour or so.

However, he decided not to risk the chance that the rancher might decide to leave a bit early. Waving good night to Boyer, he left the Blue Bell, and hurried to Shadow's stable. He cinched up quickly, led the big black out and mounted.

"A little night work, which you like," he remarked as he swung into the saddle. "And, horse, now I'm willing to bet my last peso that my hunch is a straight one. Yes, I'll wager that holed-up in the brush atop that ridge is a gent contemplating a nice juicy murder. And if we can have the luck to take the sidewinder alive, we may be able to induce him to do a little talking to save his own neck."

At a good pace, Slade rode steadily west until he reached the beginning of the ridge, where he turned north and then west. This time he hugged the shadowy edge of the growth at the base of the sag.

With his unerring instinct for distance and direction, he reached the point where he ascended the rise earlier in the evening. For minutes he sat listening and peering, heard nothing, saw nothing. Concluding he had not been spotted, he concealed Shadow and stole up the slope, as noiselessly as a drifting cloud.

It was a brilliant night of stars, but under the spreading foliage of the chaparral it was very dark. Often *El Halcón* paused to peer and listen before resuming his slow climb.

Without anything having happened, he reached the crest. He was confident that the drygulcher was lurking nearby, but exactly where, he had no idea, and if the fellow caught sight of him first, there was a very good chance that his worries would be over—so far as this world were concerned.

Still nothing happened, and he had just about decided to move east a little, as a first try to locate the hellion, when from a very short distance to the west came a sound—a faint, musical jingle of bit irons as a horse petulantly tossed its head. In utter silence he eased west.

Another moment and he saw the drygulcher, crouched at the lip of the crest, the starlight glinting on the rifle he held trained on the trail below.

A flame of wrath enveloped *El Halcón*. Yes, the scoundrel meant cold-blooded murder, no less. Had he, Slade, not played his hunch, both Dixon Lanham and Phillips would have died. He felt he was justified in mowing down the killer where he stood.

But he was a law enforcement officer and must give the devil the chance to surrender that he didn't deserve. He made sure his Colts were smooth in their sheaths, and his voice rang out, "Elevate! You're covered! In the name of the State of Texas!"

The drygulcher whirled at the sound, the rifle jutting forward. Slade drew and the two guns blazed almost as one.

Not quite. The drygulcher's slug went wild. He gave a gasping cry and slumped to the ground. Slade started forward, then hurled himself sideways to the ground as the rifle flamed a second time. The fellow, his shoulder bullet-punctured, had had the wit and the grit to play possum, but not quite quickly enough. He surged to his feet, then fell again, his breast riddled by the Ranger's slugs, the rifle dropping from his nerveless hands.

Slade stood up, felt of the bullet tear in his shirt sleeve and the slight flesh crease beneath, decided it was no importance.

"Well, I gave you your chance," he remarked to the dead man. "But you wouldn't take it. Plenty of nerve, anyhow, that I'll grant you. The side-winder sure knows how to pick 'em," he added, thinking of Alden Drake. "Hard men to the last!"

Tethered nearby, he found the outlaw's horse. He stripped off the rig and turned the animal loose, having decided to leave the body where it was for the sheriff to view. With a glance at the star-grayed trail below which, were it not for his acumen and courage, would have been darkened by blood, he descended the sag to where Shadow waited.

"Didn't work out too bad," he told the horse. "And don't go sneering at my hunches too often; sometimes they prove their worth."

Shadow, who was not given to sneering, refused to be drawn into an argument.

"Chances are we'll meet Lanham and Phillips on our way to town," his master said. "I've a notion they'll be a mite surprised."

Which was definitely in the nature of an understatement.

He had just crossed Grundy's holding, when he spotted the two cattlemen, before they did him, of course. He chuckled as he drew nearer, for each had a gun in his hand.

“Never mind any lead throwing,” he called. “I’ve dodged enough for one night.”

A volley of astonished exclamations arose. “Slade!” shouted Lanham. “What in blazes are you doing out here at this time of night?”

“Taking a little ride,” the Ranger replied as he reined in beside them. “Nice night for one.”

“Like the devil you are!” said Lanham. “You’ve been mixed up in something. Please tell us what.”

Slade told them briefly. They stared at him, a trifle dazedly.

“So you saved me again,” Lanham said heavily.

“Reckon he saved both of us this time,” Phillips chimed in.

“Possibly,” Slade conceded. “Please don’t mention what I told you until I give the word. I have my reasons for asking.”

“We won’t,” both promised.

“Dolores and the sheriff were both getting a bit bothered when you didn’t show up,” Lanham added. “Especially after Estevan came in for a moment and then slid out without saying anything. Alden Drake was in and asked if you were around. The sheriff told him he left you at the Blue Bell.”

“Which was true,” Slade interpolated. “Well, you might as well amble on home; nothing more to bother your head about tonight.”

“With you and Estevan looking after us, there never is,” Lanham declared with emphasis.

"*Gracias, muchas gracias*, as Estevan would say."

Although dawn was not very far off when he reached town, Slade did not pause in Brownsville but continued across the river, for he felt pretty sure the sheriff would be awaiting him there.

He was, with Dolores keeping him company and both looking worried. Immediately, Estevan drifted in and joined them. The story of the night's events was repeated for their benefit.

Dolores sighed, the sheriff rumbled under his mustache, and Estevan appeared pleased.

"So you see how important what you learned proved to be," Slade told him.

Estevan bowed, and remarked, "The Señor Drake rode across to his hotel and no doubt to bed, pleased with the work good of the night."

"He won't be so pleased when I pack the carcass in tomorrow," Calder growled. "I came darn near plugging the sidewinder when he asked if you were around, Walt."

"Would have been a mistake, as twelve gentlemen in a jury box would quite likely have insisted," Slade replied. "Drake's reputation is that of a respectable lawyer and businessman, and, unfortunately, we as yet have no proof to the contrary."

"That's all right," said the sheriff. "I'll still see a gent patting him down with a spade."

Dolores exclaimed over Slade's bullet-grazed

arm and wanted to apply medication at once.

"Let it go until later," Slade said. "Would attract attention and I prefer that nobody has an inkling of what happened until Tom brings in the body."

"Then suppose we call it a night," Dolores suggested.

To which nobody objected.

18

The following afternoon, Slade and the sheriff, accompanied by Estevan, the two deputies and a pack mule, rode to fetch in the body. They found the dead outlaw right where Slade had left him.

"The *ladróne* with whom the Señor Drake spoke," Estevan said, after a glance.

"Don't that sorta tie up Drake with what happened?" asked Calder.

"Not necessarily," Slade replied. "He has a right to talk with anybody he wishes, and it is not illogical that, as a lawyer, he should hold converse with dubious characters in need of legal advice. He would slip out of that loop with no difficulty."

" 'Pears keeping Dixon Lanham alive is something of a chore," commented the sheriff.

"Yes, too darn much of a chore," Slade agreed. "I've a notion that Drake is getting a mite frantic. And it is absolutely necessary to the success of his scheme that Lanham be eliminated. Well, I have a little ace in the hole I intend to play."

The drygulcher's horse, a good looking animal, was found nosing about nearby, cropping the sparse grass that grew under the chaparral. Slade glanced at the brand and shook his head.

"Mexican skillet-of-snakes burn," he said.

"Quite likely stolen from somewhere south of the river; means nothing."

"Ornery looking scut," remarked Deputy Webley, gazing at the body.

"About on a par with the others we've packed in," Slade said. "More intelligent than the average, and a hard man, as he proved when, with a hole through the top of his shoulder, he still came close to giving me my comeuppance."

Estevan picked up the fellow's rifle and examined it. "A good weapon," he remarked.

"Keep it as a souvenir," Slade said. Estevan grinned and tucked it under his arm.

"Attempted a drygulching that didn't work," Slade replied to questions when they reached Brownsville shortly after sunset. He tried to give the impression that he had been the killer's intended victim, and this was accepted without question.

After the office was cleared and the door locked, Walt Slade wrote and mailed a short letter, which the night express would convey to Laredo two-hundred miles up the Rio Grande.

And in doing this, *El Halcón* played his "ace-in-the-hole" in the case in which Dixon Lanham was concerned.

He had hesitated to write the letter because of a certain possibility involved, but had finally deeded to risk it, feeling that if he read his man aright, it might well precipitate a showdown between Alden Drake and himself. Which he would welcome.

He considered the showdown extremely important. So far he had been able to foil the killer, but the law of averages said that could not continue indefinitely.

"Several more loafers were in to look at the carcass," Calder remarked when Slade had returned from posting the letter. "Seemed to think the outlaw bunch was just about finished and there was no need to pay them any further mind."

"Admirable optimism, but, I fear, a trifle premature," Slade replied. "They'll very likely be singing a different song after the devils cut loose some place, as I predict they will, and soon."

"Oh, well, maybe we can get the jump on 'em," Calder said cheerfully. "Meanwhile, suppose we go eat. Suppose you'll be crossing the bridge later?"

"Probably," Slade conceded. "Feel I can do more over there than here."

"Been sorta working out that way, I'll have to admit," agreed the sheriff. "Let's mosey."

In the Blue Bell, the latest outlaw debacle was the subject of optimistic discussion. Even Fats Boyer, who should have known better, was inclined to believe there was little more to worry about. "Just Mr. Slade being on the job is enough to send what's left of the horned toads skalleyhootin'," he declared.

Slade thanked him for the compliment, but was not impressed.

"One thing is sure," the sheriff observed as they waited for their order to be served, "you're sure thinning 'em out. If you were right when you said, after the hotel robbery, that Drake had only three wind spiders left, now he's got only two."

"Yes, but with he himself to make three, that's still enough to make plenty of trouble," Slade replied.

They enjoyed a leisurely dinner without interruption, after which they smoked and talked for a while, discussing various possibilities which might furnish the outlaws with opportunity. But then arrived at no satisfactory conclusion.

"So darn many things the hellions can take a whack at," Calder grumbled. "Maybe they'll make a try for another steamboat."

"If they do, they'll have us distinctly at a disadvantage," Slade said. "Quite a few boats on the river, and a two-hundred mile stretch between here and Laredo. Would take some shrewd guessing to figure out which one would attract them. I still contend that frustrating the attempt on that one at the Los Indios ford was very much of a fluke; we were looking for cows and we corraled a ship."

"Twirl a wide enough loop and you're pretty sure to tie onto something," the sheriff replied cheerfully.

"Okay, if you've got steamboats on the brain, suppose you have a little talk with the management here in Brownsville and learn if any particular boat is packing money."

"I'll do that," Calder promised. "Might come up with something."

Slade thought it unlikely, but it wouldn't hurt to try. He had something of a somewhat similar nature in his own mind, but not relative to river steamers. He glanced at the clock. "I think I'll walk across the bridge," he announced. "Suppose you remain here for a while, on the chance of something cutting loose on this side of the river."

"Okay," Calder agreed. "I'll see you later."

Although very much on the alert, Slade sauntered slowly through the streets and across the span, for if anybody had designs on him, he was determined to provide every opportunity to put them into effect, confident of his ability to take care of anything that might be attempted.

A foolhardy course, perhaps, but he was in a reckless mood, being heartily weary of the continued suspense and the so far fruitless endeavor to anticipate what the outlaws might have in mind.

Reaching Matamoros without incident, he wandered about the Plaza de Hidalgo for some time. A little later he paused before the *Casa Mata*, where there had been many executions during the various revolutions.

The grim fortress interested him. A large dome used as a lookout post rose above the flat roof. The second-story walls were pierced by openings for rifle barrels.

The sinister building was ideal for a drygulcher, if he knew his intended victim would pass that way.

However, the gloomy structure remained silent, to all appearances deserted. Which was not surprising, there being little to attract the curious and the citizens of Matamoros, or at least a large portion of them, especially among the more superstitious, believed the old shack rested under a curse and was the lurking place of a malevolent spirit waiting to pounce on the unwary.

Leaving the *Casa Mata* to look after its own spirits, malevolent or otherwise, he made his way to La Luz, where there was also a plentitude of spirits, ready to pop out at the pop of a cork.

Feeling somewhat frustrated by his failure to lure the outlaws into a possible lead-trading session, he ordered a drink and sat sipping it moodily, regarding the colorful scene with an unappreciative eye.

Quickly, however, his sense of humor came to the rescue and he chuckled.

"The mountain labored and didn't even bring forth a mouse," he misquoted to his glass. "Well, they say that all things come to him who waits, so we'll just settle down and do a little waiting amid pleasant surroundings."

To further help matters, Dolores, gay and vivacious, soon joined him. They exchanged a few quips, danced a couple of numbers.

Estevan strolled in, shook his head slightly; apparently he had nothing to report.

Amado appeared, bearing his inevitable bottle and his crystal glasses. He poured the golden wine before speaking. "The small one with the hair like a forest pool with sunset filled I fear I shall lose," he remarked. "The Señor Lanham will her bear away. *Ai*! The wife she is cut out to be rather than the girl of the dance floor. It is well."

"I think so, too," Slade said. "How about you, Dolores?"

"As I said the other night, Juanita is lucky," the blue-eyed girl replied, and the blue eyes were just a trifle wistful.

"And lucky that the good deed *Capitán* again did last night," Amado added.

Business was good in the cantina, and getting better, for several of the town establishments had paid their workers that day and folks had money in their pockets that was itching to be spent. Amado hurried back to the far end of the bar, next to the till, the bell of which was playing a merry tune. Dolores scampered to the dance floor. Estevan slid out, no doubt to "watch and listen." Slade sat with his coffee and cigarettes. He was feeling better, but the vague presentiment of trouble in the making persisted. And he was growing increasingly restless.

Finally he gave up. Waving to Dolores, he left the cantina. Outside he breathed deep of the clean, fresh air, pleasant after the smoke and the noise.

Again he stood and gazed at the *Casa Mata*. The grim building seemed to leer at him derisively, the rifle slits in the wall were as mocking eyes. With a mutter, he turned and made his way to the Plaza de Hidalgo, where there was a cheerful contrast of bustle and orderly confusion. Everything appeared to be under control, with no signs of disturbance. He wandered about among the shops and bazaars for a while, then gradually worked toward the bridge approach. Here, too, all appeared peaceful.

And then the peaceful hush of the waterfront was shattered by a sound on the north side of the river, a mournful whistle wail that broke into a series of staccato notes, such as was used as a fire alarm.

He could see no sign of smoke or flame, but that blasting whistle said something wasn't right on the north bank of the Rio Grande. He went up the approach at a fast pace, reached where the span levelled off. The bridge was undergoing some minor repairs, and there were low stacks of planking scattered about against the rail.

The whistle continued to wail, and abruptly it was punctuated by still another ominous sound, a crackle of gunfire that ceased as suddenly as it began, and was followed by a thunderous beat of horses' irons on the planking, swiftly drawing nearer.

Under one of the tall lamps, three speeding horsemen loomed. A shout of alarm, then a blaze of guns as Slade dived for the shelter of the nearest low pile of lumber. He whipped out both Colts and let drive, left and right as the riders, hat brims pulled low, neckerchiefs up high, flickered toward him.

One of the riders spun from the saddle and to the floor of the bridge. Slade's fingers tightened on the triggers.

Lights blazed before his eyes, bell notes stormed in his ears. He slammed against the heap of lumber and slid to the floor, blood streaming down his face from where a slug had grazed his temple. More slugs whizzed toward him as the two remaining horsemen flashed past, but did not connect.

With the aid of the lumber pile, he managed to scramble erect, reeling and staggering like a drunken man from the shock. His vision clearing a little, he saw the two riders swerve right at the foot of the approach, go tearing through the outskirts of the town and west on the Camino Real.

The whistle had ceased blasting, but from the north side of the river drifted shouts and yells. Shaking his head to free his brain of cobwebs, his strength returning, Slade headed for the north shore, sparing the dead man on the floor boards but a passing glance that assured him he was not the one he hoped him to be; Drake had escaped again.

Regaining his normal composure, and swabbing the blood from his face with his neckerchief, he sped down the incline and reached the foot of the north approach. A short distance up-river was a crowd of excited men, grouped around the lowered gangplank of a big steamer, some streaming up the plank.

"Sure they got it," Slade heard a voice shout, "Cleaned the safe of every last blankety-blank cent! Captain's killed, I think."

19

Shouldering through the crowd, not at all gently, those who recognized him making way for him, Slade reached the gangplank and mounted it to the steamer's deck.

One glance told him the sheriff's conjecture, spoken half in jest, was justified; the outlaws did make a play for another steamboat, this time with success.

There were plenty of people on the deck, chattering, exclaiming, but only a few in the captain's lighted cabin. Slade entered at once.

The skipper lay on the floor, blood still trickling from an ugly gash in the side of his head just above the hairline. Slade knelt beside him, felt of his pulse and found it fairly strong. "Send for the doctor," he said over his shoulder.

"Done sent for him," replied a capable-looking person in uniform. "I'm the mate, Mr. Slade."

El Halcón nodded. With a clean handkerchief, he deftly padded the wound and secured it in place with his bloody neckerchief. "That should hold him until the doctor arrives," he said. "Did they get much?"

"Quite a lot, I don't know the exact amount," replied the mate. "Money consigned to Laredo. The irrigation people up there are paying off their workers, or most of them; giving them a bonus, too, I heard. Yes, the swabs did all right by themselves."

"Any notion just what happened?" Slade asked.

"Crew on shore leave," the mate answered. "I was in the hold, checking an invoice. Had just about finished when I heard steps on the deck overhead. Didn't think anything of it, just thought some of the hands had come back. When I got topside, I saw those three devils running out of the cabin. Knew something wasn't right. I grabbed the whistle cord and began sounding off to call help. Another minute and I heard a lot of shooting over toward the bridge. Kept playing the whistle. Heard some more shooting, sounded like it came from the bridge. I let go the cord and looked into the cabin. Saw the skipper on the floor, the safe open."

"Figure the captain had opened it?"

"Think he did," said the mate, "he was working on his books. If it wasn't already open, the devils did a mighty fast job of opening it. Say, you need a doctor, too; your face is all bloody."

"Just a scratch," Slade belittled his injury. "Knocked me silly for a minute, but that is all."

"Looks like more than a scratch to me," the mate said dryly.

"Here comes the doctor, and the sheriff, too," somebody shouted.

The pair, both breathing hard, entered together.

“So, beat me to it again, eh, Walt?” remarked the doctor. “How is he?”

“Not too bad, I’d say,” Slade replied.

“Any indications of fracture?”

“Not so far as I could ascertain,” the Ranger answered.

“Then there ain’t any,” Doc said conclusively. “Those fingers of yours miss nothing. Okay, I’ll give him a stimulant and tie him up neat. Should bring him out of it in a little while.”

Slade addressed Calder. He had been waiting for the doctor to finish. “Good guess,” he said, nodding toward the safe.

The sheriff seemed to understand. “But not soon enough,” he said. “Didn’t get a chance to talk with the steamboat company manager.”

“Same on my part,” Slade conceded. “I didn’t get a chance to see the bank president, as I planned to do tomorrow, and request him to keep me informed of any large withdrawal. ’Pears we’re both pretty good at hindsight, but poor where foresight is concerned.”

“Where were you dealt into the game?” Calder asked. “I see you got nicked.”

Slade told him about what had happened on the bridge.

The sheriff said several things, but registered approval. “Another souvenir for me, eh,” he remarked. “Okay, I’ll have some of these work dodgers pack the carcass from the bridge to the office. Guess that leaves only one, or two at most, right?"

"So I presume, although I'm not sure," Slade replied. "But anyway, there's still one in particular too many."

"Get a look at the varmints?"

Slade shook his head. "Not enough of a one to mean anything," he said. "Faces just vague blurs. One was tall."

"So I figured," said Calder. "Well, the deputies are outside. I'll let them take care of the chore of packing the hellion to the office. Guess you are ambling back across the river, right?"

"As soon as the captain recovers consciousness and I have a word with him," Slade replied.

"Okay, I'll walk with you," Calder said. "Saw Estevan circulating through the crowd outside. Looked to be in a bad temper. Reckon he is, not having had the luck to get in on the ruckus."

Under the doctor's ministrations, the captain did recover consciousness shortly, but could add little to what was already known. After he was helped to a chair and given a cigarette Slade rolled for him, he said, "Was working at my desk. Heard a noise behind me and started to turn around. Saw a big tall, whiskered sculpin bearing down on me under a full head of steam. Then the roof fell in. Don't remember anything else."

"Was the fact that you were carrying a large

amount of money in the safe generally known?" Slade asked.

The skipper shrugged. "Wasn't supposed to be, but I reckon one lubber too many found out," he replied. With which *El Halcón* did not disagree.

"Now you," Doc broke in turning to Slade. "Let's have a look at your noggin. A little salve and a strip of plaster and you'll be okay; couldn't crack that skull of yours with anything short of dynamite. Here's your neckerchief. It and your shirt will need a mite of rinsing; sorta spotted."

"Just wait till his little gal across the river gets a look at him," chuckled the sheriff. "There'll be the devil to pay."

"You go to bed and tomorrow you'll be all hunky-dory save for a sore top piece," Doc told the skipper.

"I've sent for the company manager and he'll take over here," the mate put in.

"That'll be fine," Slade said. "Okay, Tom, suppose we get going."

As they followed the deputies up the approach, Calder remarked, "Well, the chief hellion ought to be quite well heeled now, with two good hauls."

"Yes, he should be," Slade agreed soberly.

There was a straggle of idlers around the body when they reached it, none of whom would admit having seen the fellow in life, but 'lowed he was a mean-looking cuss. Nothing outstanding about him, was Slade's opinion. And neither he nor the sheriff nor the deputies could recall having looked on the hard-lined face before. Estevan, who glided in beside them, also shook his head.

"Doesn't really matter anyhow," Slade said.

Leaving the deputies to dispose of the body and care for the outlaw's horse, that stood patiently nearby, Slade and Calder, with a very disgruntled Estevan, headed for La Luz.

"Guess the skipper was lucky, just getting pistol whipped 'stead of being knifed," the sheriff observed.

"Yes, as in the case of the hotel robbery, they were anxious not to kick up a racket until they had tied onto the money," Slade answered. "Once they were off the boat, they didn't care, and threw some lead past folks on the street just to discourage pursuit. The mate was fortunate, too. Had he hit the deck a couple of seconds sooner, the chances are he'd have gotten a slug through him."

"The hyderphobia skunks don't know the meaning of mercy," Calder growled.

When they reached the cantina, Dolores forthwith marched Slade to the back room, where she sponged off his face and insisted he discard the blood-stained neckerchief, giving thanks the while that there was nothing more serious to contend with.

"Sometimes I think the sheriff is right when he

says some special devil of your own goes along to look after you," she observed. "No, I don't believe that's it. Much more likely it's the prayers of good people, that also always accompany you."

In this respect, Walt Swade rather believed she was right.

"Fairly presentable again, aside from that so-and-so shirt," she said, standing back with her hands on her hips and looking him over. "Now some steaming-hot coffee and you should make out. How does your head feel?"

"Had done forgot all about it," he replied cheerfully.

As he sat sipping coffee, Calder remarked, "And you feel sure the tall hellion with the whiskers was Drake?"

"Of course," Slade answered. "Drake wearing his false beard. Looks like he's getting a bit reckless, but sometimes recklessness pays off, as it did in this instance. It was him, all right, and we're not through with him yet, even though it does look like he has only one follower left."

"And I reckon we won't be until he's six feet underground," grumbled the sheriff. "Well, just a matter of time. See your gal is on her way to the dressing room. Figure she's going to head you across the bridge. It is getting late. We'll stop at the office and tell the boys to lock up, and we'll look that carcass over tomorrow. I for one am all set to call it a night."

The following afternoon, Slade and the sheriff examined the body of the slain outlaw. His pockets disgorged nothing of importance save a fair amount of money. His saddle pouch contained only some spare clothing.

"Very likely Drake carried the steamer loot," Slade remarked. "I doubt if he trusts anybody overly much."

"Not even himself," growled Calder. "Betcha he steals from one pocket and puts it in another. Well, as I said last night, the hellion must be sorta well heeled now."

"Yes, he must be," Slade agreed. "Not too far, money-wise, from being in a position to achieve his objective. Which means it's up to me to make a few fast moves, Lanham being in greater danger than ever."

"But if Lanham was done in and then Drake bought his holding, wouldn't that sorta point suspicion toward him?" the sheriff asked.

"Not necessarily," Slade replied. "It is common knowledge that Drake and Lanham talk together, and not illogical to assume that Drake advised him to make a will with his sister named as beneficiary; lawyers frequently advise their clients to that effect. So Drake knowing the sister's name, whereabouts, and her husband's type of employment would not occasion comment. And Drake, as well as being a lawyer, is also considered a land speculator. Oh, he's clever enough to cover his tracks. He's certainly been able to cover them nicely so far."

"He'll wish he'd made tracks away from here before you're finished with him," Calder predicted.

"Hope you're right," Slade smiled.

"Was I ever wrong?" said the sheriff.

Doc Beard and his coroner's jury filed in and an inquest was held on the dead outlaw. The verdict was to the effect that the blankety-blank should have gotten it long before he did. Court was adjourned.

"Steamboat skipper is okay and back on the job," Doc replied to a question from Slade. "Incidentally," he added, "he happens to be the company manager's brother-in-law. The manager told me he aimed to drop in and thank you for looking after him."

The manager did put in an appearance a little later. "Seems we keep getting deeper in your debt, Mr. Slade," he said. "If somebody, including myself, had had the brains to inform you that boat was packing the money consignment, I figure you'd very likely have saved it, just as you did the one on the downriver boat the other night.

"Incidentally, we wished to make a substantial monetary acknowledgment of our gratitude for that, but the sheriff said not to try it, that we'd just be wasting our time. Don't you think you could change your mind, Mr. Slade?"

The Ranger smilingly shook his head. "To have been able to render assistance was reward enough," he replied.

"Well, if myself or my company is ever in a position to do you a favor, please don't hesitate an instant to ask," said the manager.

Slade spent the remainder of the afternoon wandering about town, learning nothing he considered of importance.

There were no signs of Alden Drake, which did not surprise him much. But he made it a point to pass the lawyer's office. It was unoccupied, the door shut.

After spending a while with Burley Sturm and Teresa, he watched the sunset, then repaired to the Blue Bell, where he and the sheriff had their evening meal together. Dixon Lanham wasn't coming to town for a couple of days, so he didn't have him to worry about.

At La Luz, later, Estevan had nothing to report, for which Dolores was grateful. Everybody called it a night quite early.

20

The next day, Slade's letter to Laredo brought results. A distinguished-looking, middle-aged gentleman descended from the noon train, asked directions to the sheriff's office, and proceeded there without delay.

When he entered, Slade rose smiling to greet him, and they shook hands with the warmth expected of old friends.

The gentleman was Ernest Clark, Chief Construction Engineer for the Bright Alexander Company, who was putting the finishing touches to the great Laredo irrigation project. He was deeply indebted to Slade for several things, including his life.

The sheriff was introduced. Clark sat down, accepted a cup of coffee and grinned at Slade. "Well, Walt, got something good to tell me?" he asked.

"I venture to trust you will think so," the Ranger replied.

"If you say so, there's no doubt about it," Clark declared emphatically and looked expectant.

"You and I will take a little ride after a bit," Slade told him. "The sheriff will round you up a horse."

Clark chuckled and stretched out a foot. "I

anticipated that," he said. "See, I'm wearing riding boots."

After talking with Calder for a while, they set out, heading west on the Laredo trail. Clark chatted about the Laredo project and other things of interest to both, but Slade was mostly silent, constantly scanning their surroundings, although he hardly expected any untoward happening.

Without incident, they reached the point on Lanham's holding where the overflow of past ages had taken place, and where was located the great hollow that had so interested Slade when he'd first viewed it. "Well, here you are," he told the engineer. "For untold centuries the Rio Grande has deposited silt on this lowland. In consequence, the soil under the grass is exceedingly rich, requiring only water to make it immensely productive. And over there is a natural impounding basin that will require a minimum of work to put in proper shape. What do you think?"

The engineer whistled. "I think, no, I'm positive we will want this land, Walt, every acre of it. Do you think you can persuade the owner to sell? Cattlemen are often so darn obstinate and contrary, reluctant to part with a furlong of their holdings for love or money. Remember the trouble we had at Laredo, which you finally ironed out. The company will be glad to pay a very large price for all this bottoms land. Do you think you can get him to sell?"

"I'm sure I can," Slade answered. "Like to ride up to his *casa*, it isn't far, and have a talk with him?"

"Fine!" said Clark. "Let's do that."

They rode slowly. The engineer, producing pencil and paper, let the knotted reins fall on his horse's neck and took copious notes as they rode, his enthusiasm growing. "Walt," he said, "it seems you are always doing folks big favors. Just wait until I tell Alexander about it, he's at Laredo for the time being and will be there when I get back. He'll be wiring old Jaggers Dunn without delay, and Dunn will be as pleased as I am."

"Hope so," Slade returned smilingly, "he's a fine old jigger."

When they reached the Bar L *casa*, they found Lanham at home. The horses were led to the barn and oats, and they entered the living room, Lanham shouting to the cook to prepare coffee and a snack. Clark was introduced and after a bit of casual conversation, broached the matter that had brought him to the ranchhouse.

Lanham looked a trifle bewildered. "Why, I never thought of such a thing," he said.

Clark wrote on the paper, raised his eyes. "Mr. Lanham," he said, "of course this will have to be confirmed by Mr. Alexander, the president of my company, but I anticipate no difficulty. Here is approximately the sum my company will pay for those bottoms lands."

Lanham stared at the figures, his eyes widening. He turned to Slade. "What—what do you say, Walt?" he asked, his voice shaking a trifle.

"I say accept Mr. Clark's offer," *El Halcón* instantly replied.

Lanham drew a deep breath, then chuckled. "Looks like I can retire my cows to pasture to live out their lives in peace and comfort," he said. Both his hearers laughed.

"That's a notion, all right," Slade said. "They deserve a break."

"Okay, it's a deal," Lanham said.

"I'll have the necessary papers drawn up and be back here in a few days," Clark promised. "And thank you, Mr. Lanham."

"Thank him," said Lanham, gesturing to Slade. "If it wasn't for him, I wouldn't be here to make the deal, and anyhow I wouldn't make it unless he okayed it."

"I understand exactly how you feel," Clark said. "I also have an exceedingly good reason for feeling that way. If it wasn't for him, *I* wouldn't be here either."

Lanham instinctively stretched out his hand and they shook.

After enjoying a bountiful and tasty snack, Slade and the engineer made ready to depart.

"Okay for me to ride to town with you, me and Phillips?" Lanham asked. "I'd like to tell Juanita about this."

"Okay with me," Slade agreed, not objecting to having word of the transaction spread about. But when Lanham accompanied him to the kitchen to thank the cook for the excellence of his offering, he said, "Don't start back to the spread tomorrow before seeing me."

"I won't," Lanham promised, understanding perfectly.

When they reached Brownsville, Clark glanced at his watch. "Walt," he said, "if you don't mind, I'm going to catch the evening train back to Laredo; I have time to make it. I wish to consult with Alexander as quickly as possible. I'll be seeing you in a few days."

Slade walked to the station with him, leaving Lanham and Phillips at the Blue Bell, where Estevan was keeping the sheriff company, with two of his followers at the bar; there was nothing to worry about for the moment so far as Lanham was concerned.

After seeing the engineer aboard his train, Slade returned to the Blue Bell. The Ranger having granted him permission to do so, Lanham was telling Fats Boyer of his good fortune. Slade smiled to himself. Very soon the news would be common property, which was just what he desired.

Upon Slade's arrival, Estevan and his knife men drifted out. Slade had coffee and a sandwich with the sheriff. "Well, I gambled, and I hope I played my cards right," he told the peace officer.

"I hesitated to write Clark, fearing that Drake, once he realized the jig was up and there was no chance for him to tie onto Lanham's holding, would pull out of the section and I'd have to chase him all over Texas and possibly elsewhere. Finally, however, I concluded, perhaps erroneously, although I don't think so, that he wouldn't do that, at least for a while, and took a chance, chiefly in an endeavor to keep Lanham alive. I'd say that after tonight he'll be safe."

"To my way of thinking, you did the plumb right thing," Calder said.

"Also," Slade added slowly, "I've a feeling that Drake, knowing perfectly well that I'm responsible for Lanham selling to the Alexander people, may be angry enough to try and force a showdown of one sort or another with me."

"A nice prospect for you, I must say," Calder snorted.

"I'd welcome it," Slade replied. "After all, I'm a Texas Ranger and it is my duty to bring that cold killer to justice. And as I've said many a time, if your number isn't up, nobody can put it up; so why worry? Then, there is also the chance that he'll pay me no mind, but concentrate on making one more good haul before pulling out or settling down to respectability, still completely in the clear."

"And you figure he might really settle down as a lawyer?"

"It is possible, although experience leans to the contrary," Slade replied. "I've found that it is very seldom that a person who has dedicated himself to a life of crime turns from it. The lust for easy money, and perhaps the thrill and excitement of pitting his wits against the law, as a rule, govern his actions. They usually don't change."

"And the only solution is to give the devil his comeuppance in one way or another," said the sheriff.

"Usually the case," Slade granted. "And that's why I'm cudgelling my brains in an endeavor to work up some plan that will set a trap for him, so far with no success."

"Oh, well, you're most always a jump ahead of the rapscallion, and I figure you'll keep it up," Calder said cheerfully.

"Not the last two times," Slade pointed out with a somewhat wry smile.

The sheriff repeated his favorite remark, "Just a matter of time. There are going to be a lot of surprised folks when the word gets around of what Clark and his company figure to do," he continued. "Everybody's took it for granted that there would soon be a steppin' up of irrigation to the southeast of town, but nobody paid the land over to the west any mind."

"Yes," Slade agreed, "I expect there will be many surprised people."

With seeing eyes he gazed into the future and

could envision an oasis of productive green where now was only grasslands—citrus orchards, vegetable farms, and cotton fields, eventually the city's greatest source of wealth, with prosperity, happiness and content for the many. For the Alexander Company catered to the little man, with his welfare always in mind.

Calder glanced toward the bar and chuckled.

"See Lanham is gettin' plumb fidgety," he said. "Guess he's anxious to get across the river and tell his gal how things have worked out. Shall we go?"

"Might as well," Slade replied. "We'll get the rigs on our nags. They should be rested by now and will no doubt also appreciate a change of scenery. Tell him we'll meet him outside; his critter and Phillips' are at the rack."

Slade gave their surroundings but cursory attention as they rode to Matamoros, knowing that Estevan and his bunch were clearing the path for them.

When they reached the cantina, Lanham immediately hauled Juanita from the dance floor to a table, where they engaged in animated conversation. Dolores and Amado seemed acquainted with the recent development.

"Orange blossoms!" Dolores giggled, gazing at the absorbed pair at the table. "Yes, I smell 'em. Come on, Walt, and dance with me; guess you can do that, at least."

They had not one dance but several. Slade had thrown off his somber mood and Dolores was very gay, perhaps inspired by what she was confident was in store for Juanita. For she liked the little redhead and was anxious that she should be happy.

As business was good, Dolores went on the floor for a while. Phillips was at the bar. Lanham had eyes only for his charming companion.

Estevan glided in, his eyes snapping, and made his way straight to Slade's table. "He comes!" he remarked sententiously.

"Huh! What's that?" exclaimed the sheriff.

"The Señor Drake," was the laconic response. "Across the bridge he rode. To La Luz he comes."

With this, the knife man slid away to the end of the bar.

A few minutes later, Alden Drake did in fact enter, to all appearances his usual imperturbable self. But Slade sensed a hot glow in the depths of his keen eyes. He waved a greeting to Slade and the sheriff, made his way to the bar, and ordered a drink, not even glancing toward where Lanham and Juanita sat holding hands.

"Guess he's heard about Lanham's deal with Clark," the sheriff ventured.

"He could hardly have been kept from hearing, the way the matter is being discussed everywhere," Slade replied.

"Figure he still doesn't believe you've caught onto him?" Calder asked.

"Somehow I think that's it," Slade said. "I feel he is so confident of himself that he believes he has covered up perfectly, which he has come very, very close to doing. I'm waiting for just one tiny slip. Keep your face straight; he can see your reflection in the back bar mirror."

"I will," the sheriff answered, "but it sure strains my insides to. Wonder why he is in here?"

"Perhaps for no definite reason," Slade said. "Hard to tell, though; he's as full of tricks as a tree full of squirrels."

"He'll be full of something else 'fore you're finished with him," Calder muttered. "Think he's decided to lay off Lanham?"

"No reason why he shouldn't, so far as I can see," Slade replied. "Now Lanham's death would profit him nothing, which he very well knows. Hope I'm right."

Drake didn't stay long. He had a couple of drinks, waved a cordial good night and departed.

Slade thought the sheriff would bust a cinch. "Knows very well we have nothing on him," he remarked to the peace officer. "Looked just a trifle amused."

Calder was too consumed with wrath to even reply.

The night passed without event, as Slade expected it would. The same applied to the next two days, with the sheriff growing increasingly nervous and Slade himself not pleased with the continued suspense.

And then chance, or fate, at long last was to give *El Halcón* a break and provide him with opportunity.

Around early afternoon, a blocky, well-upholstered gentleman drove a buckboard into Brownsville. On the seat beside him was a hefty satchel. A livery stable accommodated the buckboard and the horses. The gentleman, carrying the satchel, made his way to the Blue Bell, talked a little with Fats Boyer, the satchel never leaving his hand, sat down, and ordered a meal, the satchel on a chair within hand's reach.

Walt Slade, who was having a sandwich and a cup of coffee, noted him but paid him no mind. A little later, he walked to the sheriff's office to commune with Calder.

"Walt," the sheriff said, "seeing as there's nothing going on, why don't you take the evening off and ride over to old Zeke Combs' *casa* for a visit with him. He's stove up with rheumatics and ain't fit for riding. He was asking about you and wondering why you don't show up."

"Tom, that's a notion," Slade replied. "I have been neglecting my old *amigo*. Everything appears to be under control, so I'll do just that."

21

Slade rode slowly, enjoying the beauty of the afternoon, for he had plenty of time to reach Combs' ranchhouse before dark. The air was crisp with the coming of autumn. The distant hills were already flecked with scarlet and with gold. Warrior monks in serried ranks, marching to give losing battle to the white legions of the frost.

Truly a land worth dying for, and living for, Slade thought. Twice it had been gripped by the iron fingers of war, but had survived, this empire of the Southwest. Survived to grow prosperous and great. Slade was uplifted by the thought.

Not far from where the track leading to Combs' *casa* left the Laredo trail, it wound through a fairly long stand of tall and thick chaparral. Here the Ranger rode watchful and alert, as a matter of habit, for he really didn't expect anything untoward to happen.

As he neared the *casa*, Slade spotted a big bunch of cattle, fully two-hundred head, he estimated. Adding to their number and holding them in close herd, were half a dozen cowhands.

"Shovin' 'em to the loading pens in the morning," the range boss said, after they had exchanged greetings. "Yep, a big herd, and we're keeping a close eye on it."

"Always a wise thing to do, although I doubt if there's much likelihood anybody will attempt anything against them," Slade replied.

"Let 'em try it!" the range boss said grimly. "We'll be ready for 'em. The Old Man will be mighty glad to see you, Mr. Slade; he's been hoping you'd drop in."

"I would have sooner," Slade said, and rode on through the deepening dusk.

When he reached the ranchhouse, he found old Zeke hobbling about, improved, but still in no condition to fork a horse. He was delighted to see his unexpected guest and said so in no uncertain terms.

They had dinner together and then for quite a while sat talking over old times and the adventures they had shared, and they discussed Lanham's deal with the irrigation people, of which Combs heartily approved.

"I like him and am glad to hear of his good luck," Combs observed. "Figure he's going to get married, eh? That's good, too; will serve to quiet him down and keep him in one place. He's like a lot of younger owners, same as chuck-line riding cowhands, always on the move. Well, I expect the little gal will hold him in line."

Finally, Slade glanced at the clock. "Will have to be getting back to town," he announced. "Calder will be on the lookout for me. See you're shoving cows to the loading pens tomorrow."

"That's right," returned Combs. "Expect Murchison, the buyer, to show up most any time now. Chances are you'll meet him on the way in. He figured to reach Brownsville this afternoon, give his nags a chance to rest a bit, and then head for there where he'll spend the night. He's quite a card—I've done business with him for years. He has his own notions and sticks to 'em, but he's a square-shooter and dependable."

"I think I saw him in town," Slade rcmarked. "On the chunky side, with gray-streaked hair. Was carrying a big satchel."

"That's right," repeated the rancher. "Never lets it out of his hand. He packs a fortune in the old gripsack. One of his notions is to pay cash for everything, which, as you know, lots of the old-timers prefer. A check would be all right with me, but I humor him, for I don't care either way."

"I see," Slade said, his eyes narrowing slightly. "Well, I'll be moving. Will see you soon again, Uncle Zeke."

Reaching the stable, Slade cinched up with frantic speed. "Horse, it's up to you to sift sand," he told Shadow. "Otherwise a man will die tonight. Blazes! What a set-up for Drake! Plumb made to order! And I've the strongest kind of a hunch that he's going to take advantage of it. Almost certain to be pulled in the belt of thicket to the south. I only hope we're not too late. Well, we'll do what we can, and hope for the best."

As soon as he was away from the ranchhouse yard, his voice rang out, urgent, compelling, “Trail, Shadow! Trail!”

Instantly the great horse lunged forward, snorting gaily, slugging his head above the bit, and in a matter of seconds, going at top speed.

There were patches of cloud in the sky, some of them heavy, but for the most part the moon, almost directly overhead, shone brightly. Slade constantly scanned the terrain ahead, hoping against hope that the buyer would appear.

But the prairie remained lonely and deserted, with no signs of life save occasional clumps of grazing cattle. Now, far ahead, shone the belt of thicket, the twigs glowing, silvered. He reached it and rode recklessly between the stands of growth. And as he rode, he slipped from a cunningly contrived secret pocket in his broad leather belt and pinned to his shirt front the gleaming silver star set on a silver circle, the feared and honored badge of the Texas Rangers. The time for deception was past and he felt he might need the authority it represented.

From directly ahead, sounded the crack of a gunshot. Slade’s breath caught in his throat. Looked like he was too late. He sent Shadow careening around a bend in the trail, and a grim tableau was spread before his eyes.

Only a few yards distant, a buckboard was jammed against the growth. From it a man was hauling a big satchel. On the ground lay a motionless form, doubtless Murchison, the buyer. And mounted on a splendid sorrel horse was a second man who flung up his head at the thudding of Shadow's irons. The neckerchief about the lower half of his face had slipped down, and Slade instantly recognized Alden Drake. He jerked Shadow to a slithering halt, and his voice thundered through the stillness of the night, "Up! Drake! You are under arrest! In the name—"

Alden Drake gave a yell of fury. His hand flashed to his holster.

The man on the ground dropped the satchel and cleared leather first. Slade, weaving, ducking, drew and shot with both hands.

The man on the ground crumpled up to lie still. Drake blazed a bullet that fanned Slade's face. He, too, was weaving, ducking. Slade lined sights. But as he squeezed the triggers, Drake hurled himself forward on his horse's neck, whirled the sorrel, and went charging around the bend, apparently untouched.

Slade sent Shadow surging forward, flung himself from the saddle and knelt beside the buyer, giving him a moment of examination.

"Just creased, can wait," he told Shadow as he leaped erect and back into the saddle. "Trail, feller, trail!"

Again the great black lunged ahead, and the race was on!

In a matter of moments, they cleared the growth and Slade sighted Drake, now far to the front and going like the wind. He settled himself in the saddle, for it looked like the race would be a long one. Drake had a head start and in the tall sorrel, Shadow had almost, for once, met his match.

Ahead shone the gray ribbon of the Laredo Trail. Drake swerved into it and went speeding west.

The miles rolled back under Shadow's pounding irons, but the distance between him and the flying sorrel remained almost the same. Slade encouraged him with voice and hand. "You'll do it, feller, you'll do it!" he repeated over and over. "He'll never outrun you. He won't last much longer."

Slade was right. The golden horse had given his all, and it was not enough. His eyes were gorged with blood. His nostrils flared and he breathed in convulsive sobs. And behind him that black demon slowly but surely closed the distance. Slade could see the whitish blur of Drake's face as he turned to glare over his shoulder at his relentless pursuer.

Slade fingered the butt of his rifle, but he did not draw it from the boot. For he earnestly desired to take Drake alive, were it humanly possible. He knew he'd be risking his own life, but he'd chance it.

With his pursuer within easy six-gun range,

Drake gave it up, hauled his faltering horse to a halt, and jerked him around to face the Ranger, his features convulsed with insane hate. Directly below the edge of the trail, rolled the dark waters of the river.

And there on the banks of the Rio Grande they shot it out, the orange flashes gushing through the moonlight.

Slade reeled slightly as a slug touched his cheek bone. He steadied himself and fired. Drake gave a wailing cry, lurched forward, sideways, fell from the saddle on the very edge of the steep bank, and rolled down it and into the river. Slade sent Shadow to the lip of the bank.

But at that instant, one of the heavier patches of cloud drifted across the face of the moon and the light went out like a snuffed candle.

And when the cloud finally passed, the placid surface of the Rio Grande was unmarred, and the great river, as many, many times in the past, was hiding its grim secret well.

Dismounting listlessly, for abruptly he was very, very tired, Slade gazed for a moment at the dark, hurrying water. "Trail's end," he remarked to Shadow. "Or is it? Guess I'll never know for sure."

Approaching the exhausted sorrel, he removed the rig and turned the animal loose. Then he remounted and rode back the way he had come,

Shadow jogging along at a good pace, apparently little affected by the gruelling chase.

Reaching the spot where they had left the stalled buckboard, they found Murchison still lying on the ground, but rolling his head and muttering with returning consciousness. Slade knelt beside him again and a moment or two later, the buyer opened his eyes and stared dazedly at the Ranger. "What—what happened?" he mumbled.

"A couple of enterprising gents with share-the-wealth notions drygulched you and tried to tie onto your money," Slade explained. "Didn't get it—your satchel is there on the ground unopened. What's left of one of them is lying beside it. The other went into the river. Think you can sit up?"

"I—I believe I can," the buyer faltered. Slade eased him up, rolled and lighted a cigarette, and placed it between his lips. Murchison took a couple of deep drags, which evidently helped.

"Say!" he exclaimed. His voice was about back to normal. "Aren't you Mr. Slade, Sheriff Calder's deputy? Boyer was telling me about you."

"Guess that's right," Slade conceded. "Think you'll be able to drive in a little while? We'll head back to town and let the doctor give you a once-over. Take it easy now."

Securing his medicants, he padded and bandaged the cut in the buyer's scalp, the bleeding of which had almost stopped.

"That should hold you until you see the doctor," he said. "Still think you can drive?"

The old fellow was rugged, and filled with surly courage. He 'lowed he could, were he helped to the seat. Slade eased him onto it and he gathered up the reins. The well-trained horses, which had remained right where they were, moved back along the trail.

"Never mind about Combs," Slade told the buyer. "He'll just think you were delayed in town."

Murchison profusely expressed his gratitude to the Ranger. "Figure I owe you my carcass as well as my money," he said. "I've a notion the scoundrels would never have left me alive, against the chance I might have recognized them."

Which Slade thought likely.

When they reached town, they stopped at the sheriff's office, where they found Calder and his two deputies. One cared for the buckboard and the horses, the other was dispatched to summon the doctor who, when he arrived, made light of the buyer's wound and sent him to bed.

"And you figure the sidewinder drowned in the river?" Calder asked, referring to Alden Drake's end.

"If he was hit hard enough," Slade replied.

"At least my slug walloped him out of the hull. Anyhow, this section is finished with him, which is something gained."

"You're darn right," said the sheriff. "And are a lot of folks going to be surprised!"

"It will be up to the courts to decide what disposal to make of Drake's property, of which I gather there is some," Slade remarked. "But that's out of my province, and I'm not interested."

"I'll help take care of it," Calder promised. "What next?"

"A few days rest and a talk with Ernest Clark when he returns from Laredo with the land transfer papers, then back to the Post to see what Captain Jim has lined up," Slade answered.

Three days later, Dolores said, "*Hasta luego*—till we meet again. I'll be waiting!"

Center Point Large Print
600 Brooks Road / PO Box 1
Thorndike, ME 04986-0001 USA

(207) 568-3717

US & Canada:
1 800 929-9108
www.centerpointlargeprint.com